LAMB IN THE LAUNDRY

Quietly, Mandy and James approached the ewe over the grass. Mandy knelt beside the wet little black bundle on the ground. Gently, she lifted the lamb closer to his mother.

The ewe paid no attention. Mandy tried everything. She almost pushed the poor little lamb under the ewe's nose, but it was no good. The ewe had time for only one lamb, and it wasn't this one.

It was when the ewe raised her head and gave an unmistakably angry bleat that Mandy knew it was useless.

"She's rejected him," said James.

Give someone you love a home!
Read about the animals of Animal Ark™

LAMB in the LAUNDRY

Ben M. Baglio

Illustrations by Shelagh McNicholas

Cover illustration by
Mary Ann Lasher

AN
APPLE
PAPERBACK

SCHOLASTIC INC.

New York Toronto London Auckland Sydney
Mexico City New Delhi Hong Kong

Special thanks to Helen Magee.
Thanks also to C. J. Hall, B.Vet.Med., M.R.C.V.S., for reviewing
the veterinary information contained in this book.

ISBN 0-439-08642-6

All rights reserved. Published by Scholastic Inc., 555 Broadway, New York, NY 10012, by arrangement with Working Partners Limited. ANIMAL ARK is a trademark of Working Partners Limited. SCHOLASTIC and associated logos are trademarks and/or registered trademarks of Scholastic Inc.

12 11 10 9 8 7 6 5 4 3

0 1 2 3 4/0

Printed in the U.S.A.
First Scholastic printing, September 1999

40

™

One

"Ready?" asked Dr. Adam.

"Coming," Mandy replied, smiling at her dad. "Blackie wants to carry the picnic basket."

Dr. Adam grinned. "As long as he doesn't eat all the food," he said.

"Even Blackie couldn't handle all that," said James. He pushed his glasses up higher on his nose and bent down to Blackie. Blackie was James's Labrador. "Put it down, Blackie," he said.

Blackie looked up at him and wagged his tail — but he held on to the handle of the basket.

Mandy laughed. "He isn't getting any more obedient," she said.

James brushed his hair out of his eyes. "Down, Blackie!" he said.

Blackie looked up at James sorrowfully and barked. The basket tumbled to the ground.

"Got it," Mandy said, grabbing it. She looked at Blackie. "You'll get your share of the picnic, Blackie," she said.

"Lucky there isn't anything breakable in there," said Dr. Emily.

Mandy looked at her mom, leaning through the kitchen window of the cottage.

"It's a wonder he could pick it up," she said. "What did you put in here, Mom?"

Emily Hope laughed and her green eyes danced. Her red hair shone in the sun. "Oh, this and that," she said. "Enough to keep three hungry people happy."

"And a hungry dog," James said, grabbing Blackie's collar before he could get to the basket again.

"Enough to feed an army," said Dr. Adam as he got into the car. "Come on. We don't have all day."

Dr. Emily laughed. "But that's exactly what you have," she said. "A whole day to wander on the moors and have a picnic."

Mandy turned to her mother. "It's a shame you can't come, Mom," she said.

Emily Hope shook her head. "Somebody has to watch the clinic," she said. "And it's been ages since your dad has had a day off."

"And I'm going to make the most of it," Adam Hope said. "Get in, you two — three," he added, looking at Blackie.

Mandy and James got into the car. Blackie bounded after them.

"Have a good time," Dr. Emily called.

Jean Knox, the clinic receptionist, appeared at the window beside her. "Enjoy yourselves," she said.

Mandy looked back as the car drove out of Animal Ark's driveway. Dr. Emily and Jean waved from the kitchen window. It was a lovely sunny morning and Mandy wished her mom could have come with them. She sighed.

Dr. Adam turned his head. "Someone has to take care of the animals," he said.

Mandy nodded. Animal Ark was a busy veterinary practice and both her parents were vets. They didn't have much free time. And Mom was right: it had been ages since Dad had had a day off.

"It's going to be wonderful," Mandy said.

Dr. Adam laughed. "That's the spirit!" he said. "I'm looking forward to this picnic."

"So is Blackie," James said.

Mandy gave the Labrador a hug. "First you have to do a little walking," Mandy said. "Then we eat."

Blackie wagged his tail and jumped up, knocking James's glasses off.

"Blackie!" said James, laughing.

Blackie wasn't the most obedient dog in the world — or the best behaved — but he was a lot of fun.

"Where are we going?" James asked as he settled his glasses back on his nose.

Mandy turned around to point out of the car window to the moor above Welford village. "Up there," she said. "Black Tor."

"Terrific," said James. "It's been a long time since I've been to Black Tor."

The car swung around the crossroads by the Fox and Goose pub, and Mandy and James waved to Mr. Hardy, the owner, as they passed. He looked up from rolling a barrel into the pub and waved back.

Then they were out of the village and climbing toward the moor. Mandy loved the moor. It could be wild and windy in winter, and the snow could pile itself into drifts four feet deep. But today, in the spring sunshine, it looked perfect.

The car climbed higher and Mandy and James looked back. Welford lay spread out below them. They could see Animal Ark, the old stone cottage at the front and the modern extension that housed the clinic at the back. They spotted James's house at the other end of the village and Mandy's grandparents' cottage with their trailer home sitting outside. And behind the Fox and Goose was the lane where Walter Pickard and Ernie Bell lived, both church bell ringers like Grandpa. Then there was the church and the post office and the town hall.

"It looks like a toy village," James said.

"Look," said Mandy. "You can see Walton. There's the school." Walton was the neighboring town, two miles from Welford.

"Ugh!" groaned James. "Don't mention school. Not when vacation just started!"

"And there's the cottage hospital," Mandy said, pointing to a long, low building on the outskirts of Walton. It was the little local hospital for Walton and Welford. "Grandma says there's a new head nurse there now."

James nodded. "I know," he said. "Johnny Pearson broke his leg playing soccer. He's in the cottage hospital. Mark says he's scared stiff of the head nurse." Mark was Johnny's older brother. He was in Mandy's class at school.

Mandy made a face. "She must be bad if Johnny's afraid of her," she said. "Johnny's a nightmare."

James grinned. "Mark says it's time somebody kept Johnny in line."

Mandy turned to face the way they were going. "Look, Dad," she said. "There are lambs in the fields already."

Dr. Adam's beard twitched as he smiled. "As if I didn't know," he said. "How many calls did I have last week?"

"Oops, sorry!" Mandy said. The Hopes were always very busy at lambing time.

James was looking out of the side window. "Mrs. McFarlane was saying that somebody moved into Fordbeck Farm," he said.

The McFarlanes ran the Welford post office. Mrs. McFarlane knew everything that was going on, almost before it happened.

Dr. Adam nodded. "The Spillers," he said. "I've been in to see them a couple of times."

"The people with the little girl?" asked Mandy.

Her dad nodded. "Jenny. She's six. And Mrs. Spiller is expecting another baby any day now."

"Do they have lambs?" Mandy asked.

Dr. Adam nodded again. "This is their first lambing season. The Spillers aren't country folk. Mr. Spiller lost his job and they bought that old farm. I have to hand it to Jack Spiller. He's doing a good job. Only thing is, they can't afford to pay anybody to help them, so he has to do it all himself."

Mandy opened her mouth to ask why Mrs. Spiller didn't help. She was so used to her mom and dad working together, sharing the load. Then she remembered the new baby.

"That must be hard at lambing time," James said.

Dr. Adam gave him a smile. "That's why I thought you wouldn't mind if we stopped in on the way to Black Tor. Just to see how they're doing."

Mandy grinned. Typical. If her dad thought someone needed a hand he would be there — day off or no day off.

"I'd love to see some lambs," Mandy said.

Dr. Adam glanced at Blackie, but James said, "No need to worry. Blackie's no problem around sheep. He's as gentle as . . ."

"A lamb," Mandy finished, and they laughed.

"Down here then," Dr. Adam said, and he swung the car down a dirt track off the road.

The road was bumpy — as if it hadn't been used in a long time.

"How long have they been here?" James asked.

Dr. Adam shrugged. "About eight months," he said. "Jack Spiller has worked his fingers to the bone on that farm, trying to make it work out."

"It was pretty run-down, wasn't it?" James asked.

Dr. Adam nodded. "That's the only reason he could afford it. He put every penny he had into it. And did the work on the farm buildings himself. But you don't get too much done in winter. Let's hope things start looking up for them soon."

Mandy looked at her dad thoughtfully. It sounded as if the Spillers were having a hard time.

The car bumped and jolted its way along the road and turned in at the farmyard.

Mandy looked around. The farmhouse was the long, low, old-fashioned kind. But it had been freshly white-washed, and there were daffodils growing in half barrels at the door and pots of geraniums on the window ledge. The curtains on the windows were blue gingham, and the whole place looked neat and clean.

"Needs some work done on that barn," Dr. Adam said as he stopped the car.

Mandy looked at the barn. It was true. It did look a little run-down, but there was fresh wood showing here and there where it had been mended. It was clear Mr. Spiller was working on the place.

"He started repairing it," she said. Then she saw an

old shed in the far corner of the farmyard. "Look at that," she said.

Dr. Adam looked. "That's beyond repair," he said. "That needs to be knocked down."

Dr. Adam tooted the horn. Nothing. No sign of life.

Mandy looked at the blue curtains blowing in the windows of the house. Where were the Spillers?

"Jack Spiller is probably out lambing," said Dr. Adam.

"What about Mrs. Spiller and the little girl?" Mandy asked.

Dr. Adam shook his head. He looked worried.

"Maybe you should go inside," James said to him. "The door is open."

Dr. Adam hesitated. He wasn't the type to go barging into people's houses without asking. But Mandy could see he was concerned.

Just then a little girl emerged from the house. Her dark hair was tied in ponytails with bright red ribbons. The ribbons matched her red jumper and red rubber boots. She stood on the doorstep looking at them.

"Look," said Mandy.

"That's Jenny," Dr. Adam said.

Mandy scrambled out of the car and walked slowly across the farmyard. The little girl looked scared to death. Mandy didn't want to frighten her any more.

"Hello," she said as she got nearer. "You're Jenny, aren't you?"

The child nodded but didn't say a word.

Mandy smiled encouragingly. "Where's your mom?" she asked.

Jenny turned her face up to Mandy and her eyes filled with tears. She raised a hand and pointed into the house. "In there," she said. "She's sick. She has a tummy ache — and Daddy isn't here."

James and Dr. Adam were out of the car now.

"Dad?" said Mandy.

Dr. Adam's face looked worried. "I heard," he said quietly. "Keep Jenny out here while I go and see what's wrong."

And he strode into the house.

Mandy and James looked at each other. Jenny's face was streaming with tears now. Mandy reached an arm out to give her a hug, but then Blackie bounded up and began to lick the little girl's face.

It was like magic. At once the tears disappeared.

"Oh!" said Jenny. "Is he yours?"

"He's mine," James said. "His name is Blackie."

Jenny put her hand out to pet the Labrador. "He's pretty," she said. "Can I play with him? Daddy doesn't let me play with Jess."

"Of course you can play with him," James said. Then he turned to Mandy. "Who's Jess?" he asked.

Mandy shrugged her shoulders. Things at Fordbeck Farm were getting stranger and stranger.

It seemed like ages but it could only have been minutes before Dr. Adam came out of the house. His face looked very serious.

He drew Mandy away from Jenny and spoke in a low voice.

"Mrs. Spiller's baby is on the way, Mandy," he said. "I don't think we have much time."

"She isn't going to have it here, is she?" asked Mandy.

Dr. Adam shook his head. "I don't think that would be a good idea," he said. "Lambing is one thing, but human babies are another."

Mandy looked at Jenny playing happily with Blackie and James. James was doing a great job keeping the little girl's mind off her mother.

"Is there anything I can do?" Mandy said.

Dr. Adam nodded. "I can't leave Mrs. Spiller — just in case," he said. "Jack Spiller is in the top field, lambing. Go and get him."

Mandy's mind raced with questions, but one look at her dad's face told her there was no time.

"Tell him to get back here right now," said Dr. Adam. "He has to get his wife to the cottage hospital."

Mandy froze for a moment, looking at her dad. It wasn't often he was so abrupt. He looked really worried.

"Run!" her dad said.

Mandy turned on her heels and ran for the top field.

Two

Mandy ran like she had never run before. It *would* be the top field, she thought. The one farthest away from the farmhouse. Her breath rasping in her throat, she scrambled over a drystone wall and raced over the field. She looked up. There, outlined against the sky, she could see the figure of a man. He was bending over a sheep. It had to be Jack Spiller.

"Mr. Spiller!" she shouted.

But the wind whipped her voice away. Panting, Mandy raced on. "Mr. Spiller!" she called again as she came closer.

The tall, dark-haired figure straightened up and turned around. A flowing black-and-white shape rose up from the grass and streaked toward her.

"Jess!" Mr. Spiller cried, and at once the shape halted and turned. Jess was a sheepdog.

Mandy stumbled the last few feet and stood looking up at the farmer, out of breath.

"Mr. Spiller," she said again.

He was a tall man with a kind face and worried eyes. He looked down at her, puzzled.

"That's me," he said. "Who are you?"

"Mandy Hope," Mandy said.

The man's face cleared. "The vet's daughter?" he asked, and smiled.

Mandy nodded. Her breath was coming back now. She reached out a hand and tugged at Jack Spiller's sleeve.

"You have to come," she said. "Back to the farm. It's your wife . . ."

At once his smile disappeared. "Maggie?" he said. "What's wrong? Did she have an accident?"

Mandy shook her head. "No," she said. "But the baby is coming. Dad says she needs to go to the cottage hospital — right away."

The words were hardly out of her mouth before Jack Spiller was off, racing down the field, leaping the dry-

stone wall as if it were nothing, running for home with
Jess beside him.

Mandy watched as he crossed the bottom field. She
hoped Mrs. Spiller would be all right — and the baby.

She felt something soft and warm nudge her leg and
looked down. A lamb, hardly a day old, blundered into
her. Mandy smiled in spite of her worry. It looked so
small and fluffy. A ewe, its mother, bleated to it, and the
lamb turned and trotted toward her. The ewe gave it a
gentle butt with its head, and the lamb drew close to its
mother's side, nuzzling for milk.

Mandy gave herself a shake. The lamb was beautiful,
but this was no time to stand there admiring it. She
turned and ran back down the hill toward the farm.

Dr. Adam was helping a young woman into a dilapi-
dated old van when Mandy arrived at the farmyard.
Jess, the sheepdog, crouched watchfully beside the
farmhouse door.

"Good job, Mandy," her dad said.

Mandy glowed with pleasure and looked at the
woman. She had short dark hair and cheeks that should
have been rosy. But now she looked pale and drawn.
She turned a worried face to Mandy.

"Thank you so much," she said. Then she looked at
Dr. Adam as she eased herself into the van. "But what
about Jenny?"

Dr. Adam looked at Mandy and James. Jenny was absorbed in talking to Blackie, kneeling beside him.

"We'll watch her," Mandy said. "Won't we, James?"

James smiled. "Of course we will," he said. "Blackie will help."

Mandy saw some of the worry fade from Mrs. Spiller's face.

Then Jack Spiller came hurtling out of the house with a bag overflowing with clothes.

Mrs. Spiller smiled. "I wasn't quite packed," she said. "The baby is a little early."

Mr. Spiller threw the bag into the back of the van. Then he turned to look at Jenny.

"Don't worry about her," Dr. Adam said. "We'll watch Jenny."

Mr. Spiller ran a hand through his hair. "I don't like asking favors," he said.

Dr. Adam smiled. "It isn't a favor," he said. "It's a pleasure. Anyway, we have to give one another a hand here in the country."

Mr. Spiller looked at him gratefully. "I'll be back as soon as I can," he said. He looked at his wife and she smiled at him.

"I'll be all right," she said. "Just drop me off at the hospital." She turned to Dr. Adam. "It's the lambing," she said. "We can't afford to get anybody to help us, and

I haven't been able to do much to help Jack recently. He just can't be away from the farm for very long."

Jack Spiller's mouth looked grim. "You've probably helped too much," he said to his wife. "I shouldn't have let you."

"Don't be silly," Mrs. Spiller said. "You can't manage it all on your own."

"I'll have to," said Jack Spiller. He turned and looked toward the top field. "There are one or two ewes I'm not happy about up there," he said. Then he gave Jess the order to stay and got into the van beside his wife.

James came and stood beside Mandy. "He can't do all that lambing on his own," he said softly.

Mandy nodded thoughtfully. "And he really should be with Mrs. Spiller at the hospital."

"What do you think?" asked James.

Mandy looked at him. "No picnic?" she said.

James shrugged. "I don't mind. There are plenty of days for a picnic."

"Not for Dad," Mandy said. "He hasn't had a day off in a long time."

"He wouldn't mind," said James.

Mandy grinned. "No, I guess not," she said.

The van engine was revving up. Jenny looked up and ran to the passenger side.

"Will you bring a baby home, Mommy?" she asked.

Mrs. Spiller smiled but Mandy saw a spasm of pain cross her face. "In a few days," she said. "Be a good girl for Daddy while I'm away."

The little girl nodded. "I'll help him," she said. "With the lambs."

"So will we," Mandy said impulsively. She turned to her father. "Won't we, Dad?"

Dr. Adam smiled. "Of course we will," he said. "I've got rubber boots in the car for everybody."

Jack Spiller's face lit up. "Really?" he asked. "You'll stay?"

"Take your time," Dr. Adam said. "We'll take care of the lambing for you — Mandy and James and I."

"And me!" said little Jenny.

Dr. Adam laughed. "And you," he said.

"I don't know what to say," Jack Spiller said. "I never expected kindness like this. You'll find the lambing bag in the top field — I hope the ewes haven't gotten at it."

Dr. Adam looked at Mrs. Spiller. Her face was very pale. "Don't worry about that," he said. "Just get going!"

The engine revved again. Mr. Spiller waved and the van was off.

"What's a lambing bag?" asked James.

Dr. Adam laughed. "It's the most important thing a shepherd or a sheep farmer has at lambing time," he said. "I'll show it to you when we find it."

"Right," said Mandy as they watched the van disappear around a bend in the road. "Let's get to work then."

"The top field, Jack said," Dr. Adam recalled. "I think we'd better take a look up there first."

"Should we take Jess?" Mandy asked.

Dr. Adam nodded. "We'll need her," he said. "Sometimes ewes can bolt and you need a sheepdog to catch them."

Dr. Adam whistled to the black-and-white collie, which came running to his heels. "Lucky Jess and I have met before," he said. "She's a good sheepdog."

"What about Blackie?" James asked.

Dr. Adam looked at the Labrador. "Better put him on the leash," he said. "I know he wouldn't harm the sheep but the sheep don't know that. A ewe panics easily at this time of year."

Jenny looked up from where she was cuddling Blackie. "Can I take him?" she asked.

James smiled. "Of course you can," he said as he clipped on Blackie's leash.

They got rubber boots and Dr. Adam's bag from the car. Then the procession started up toward the top field, Dr. Adam with Jess, Mandy and James, and Jenny with Blackie.

So much for Dad's day off, Mandy thought.

*   *   *

As they went Dr. Adam explained what needed to be done.

"We spread out," he said. "We have to check on as many ewes as possible, looking for signs of distress."

"What signs?" James said.

Dr. Adam thought for a moment. "If you see a ewe lying down, she's probably lambing. But ewes are strange creatures. They're just as likely to give birth standing up as lying down. In any case, you must keep watch to see that the lamb is born safely. Once the birth process starts it doesn't take too long."

"How do you know everything is okay?" Mandy asked.

Dr. Adam smiled. "You'll see the lamb born, then the ewe will get to her feet and start licking the lamb. Once that happens you can be sure everything will be all right."

"What if the ewe doesn't lick the lamb?" James said.

Dr. Adam frowned. "That can be difficult," he said. "You see, if the bond between mother and child isn't formed at once, you can find yourself with a rejected lamb on your hands — and a lot more work. Either you have to bring the rejected lamb into the house and hand rear it, or you have to set it on to another ewe."

"Huh?" said James.

Dr. Adam smiled. "Setting on is when you take the

skin of a dead lamb, maybe one that was stillborn, and put it on a rejected lamb. Then, if you're lucky, the mother will think it's her own lamb and feed it."

"I suppose that's better than having to hand rear a whole lot of lambs," James said, but he didn't sound too thrilled with the idea of setting on.

"It's certainly less work," said Dr. Adam.

"And Mr. Spiller is so busy already," James said. "He wouldn't have time for hand rearing. Lambs have to be fed so often when they're really young."

Dr. Adam smiled at him. "Sheep farmers don't get much time to rest during lambing. Ask any of them. And besides, it's the farmers' wives who usually do the hand rearing — in the kitchen. Now spread out," he said. "The first thing we have to do is find the lambing bag."

They spread out. Mandy was so enchanted with the little woolly lambs that skipped and hopped beside their mothers that she almost forgot what she was supposed to be looking for. It was James who shouted, "Is this it?"

Mandy looked around. James was holding up a dun-colored bag with a cord attached.

"That's it," said Dr. Adam, coming over to him. "Now you can see what's in a lambing bag."

Dr. Adam took the bag and opened it. Mandy and James and Jenny looked on as he emptied it.

"It's a sort of survival kit for sheep farmers," he said as he laid the various things out on the grass. "You see, there's string and marking fluid for identifying lambs. Then there's penicillin for giving before a difficult birth. There's lambing oil for when the farmer has to help the birth along and protein drinks for exhaustion, calcium, and a mixture for enteritis. Then the whole bag is lined with sheep's wool so that if you have to bring a lamb home it'll be cozy and warm in there."

"That's great," said Mandy.

Dr. Adam nodded. "Lambing bags are great things," he said. "Now, let's get to work."

They worked hard until midday, when Dr. Adam said they could stop and eat their picnic.

"No problems to report?" Dr. Adam asked as they settled themselves behind a drystone wall.

Mandy shook her head, her cheeks aglow as she spread the picnic on the grass beside them. There were sandwiches and crusty rolls and shiny red apples and wedges of cheese. And there were slices of fruitcake and tubs of yogurt to finish with.

"Oh, Dad, I saw a lamb being born! And it was just like you said," Mandy said.

"I saw one, too," James said. "It was tiny. It got up right away and its mother did just what you said — started licking it. Then it started to feed."

Dr. Adam laughed. "I'm glad you're enjoying it," he said.

Mandy munched on a cheese sandwich. "This is good," she said.

"Hard work makes for good appetites," Dr. Adam said.

James nodded. "It's good to sit down," he said.

Jenny looked up, her mouth full of crusty roll and cheese. "Can I give some to Blackie?" she asked.

James nodded and the little girl smiled.

"You really like Blackie, don't you?" he said.

Jenny nodded. "Dad won't let me play with Jess," she said. "I like playing with Blackie. I'd like my own Blackie."

"Working dogs aren't for playing with," said Dr. Adam. He looked around. "Where is Jess, anyway?"

Just at that moment a black-and-white shape raced over the hill and stood a few feet away, looking at them.

"Here, girl," said Mandy, but the dog stood its ground. Her head moved slightly back and forth.

At once Dr. Adam was on the alert. He stood up and the sheepdog started to move away.

"What is it, Dad?" Mandy asked.

Dr. Adam took a step forward. Jess looked back toward him and moved a few feet farther.

"I think Jess is trying to tell us something," Dr. Adam said.

Mandy scrambled to her feet. "What?" she asked.

Dr. Adam shook his head. "I don't know," he said, "but I think we'd better find out!"

Three

Jess loped in front of them, looking back now and then to see that they were following.

"Dad, you're right. She's trying to tell us something," Mandy said.

James nodded. "It looks like it."

Dr. Adam pointed. "There," he said. "Just under the drystone wall."

Mandy and James looked. A ewe lay stretched out on the ground. As they got closer Mandy could see more clearly. The ewe wasn't moving. She was lying flat on her side, her legs still, her body arched.

"Is she dead?" Mandy said.

Dr. Adam was already opening the lambing bag. "No," he said, "but there isn't much time."

"She isn't moving," said James, "and her eyes are closed."

As if the ewe had heard, she opened her eyes and gave a weak bleat.

"Careful now," said Dr. Adam. "We don't want to alarm her."

"What's wrong, Dad?" asked Mandy.

Dr. Adam bent to the ewe and ran his hands over her stiff body.

"Hypocalcemia," he said shortly.

"What's that?" asked Mandy, kneeling beside him. "Can you do something for her?"

Dr. Adam searched in the lambing bag. "It's a calcium deficiency," he said. "It sometimes happens with pregnant ewes."

"Can you cure it?" James asked.

Dr. Adam nodded. "I hope so," he said. "If it isn't too late."

Mandy saw her dad take a syringe out of the bag and a plastic bottle filled with some kind of solution.

"I have to give her an injection," he said. "Let's hope it's in time. Mandy, hold her head while I do it."

Mandy put her arms around the ewe's head. It felt

heavy and the ewe was hardly breathing. "Quick, Dad," she said. "I think she's in real trouble!"

Swiftly, Dr. Adam filled the syringe and injected the ewe.

"What now?" said James.

"Now we wait," said Dr. Adam.

"How long?" asked Mandy.

Dr. Adam smiled. "Not long," he said. "If it works."

They stood there watching the ewe as the minutes ticked by. Mandy held her breath. She thought she saw the ewe's eyes flicker. Then a tremor ran through the ewe's body and her eyes opened. The frightened animal looked up at Mandy and bleated pitifully.

"Dad?" Mandy said.

Her dad nodded. "I felt it," he said. He turned to James. "Help Mandy hold her head," he said, "and get ready to hold the ewe in case she bolts. I think I'm going to be busy at this end."

"Bolts?" asked James as he went to help Mandy.

Dr. Adam nodded. "Ewes in trouble often bolt. And with this one so close to giving birth that wouldn't be a good idea."

Mandy's eyes opened wide. "Is the lamb coming?" she asked.

Dr. Adam nodded. "Soon," he said. "But I think she'll need some help."

Mandy opened her mouth to ask more questions, but at that moment the ewe gave a shudder and began to struggle to her feet.

Mandy and James locked their arms around the ewe's neck as she stood shaking her head and pawing at the short grass. Then she gave a long bleat and strained against them.

"Hold her," Dr. Adam said urgently.

Mandy tightened her grip, talking to the frightened animal, soothing her. The ewe began to calm down.

Mandy looked at her father. He rolled his sleeves up and quickly rubbed some lambing oil on his hands and forearms. He look up briefly.

"Hold tight," he said. "Here we go."

Mandy watched as her father felt for the little creature. She saw him frown.

"What is it, Dad?"

"Twins," he said. "And they're a little mixed up in there."

Mandy bit her lip. The poor ewe's body heaved with effort and her eyes rolled upward.

"It'll all be over soon," Mandy said to her.

Another long shudder passed through the ewe's body. Mandy looked at her dad's face. He was intent on what he was doing. Then she saw him grin.

"Come on, little fellow," he said. "There's another one behind you."

And suddenly her dad's hands were full of newborn lamb as it slipped and slid on the grass. Swiftly he guided the shaking little creature around to its mother's side.

"For goodness sake, don't let her go now," he said to Mandy and James. "There's another lamb to come, and if she doesn't start licking them right way, we'll have two rejected lambs."

Mandy shifted her grasp so that the ewe could get to her lamb. She watched, breathless, as the ewe started licking the little creature clean.

"It's so tiny," she said, looking at the lamb as its mother cleaned it up.

"And here's another," Dr. Adam said, coming to stand beside her.

Mandy looked up. She had been so busy watching the first lamb, she had missed the birth of the second.

"Oh, Dad," she said as Dr. Adam put the second lamb down and the ewe began to clean that one, too. "Two lambs — and the poor ewe looked so sick!"

James grinned. "Your dad can cure anything," he said.

Dr. Adam laughed. "Hypocalcemia isn't hard to cure

if you have the right treatment. But it's Jess we have to thank. If she hadn't come to fetch us, the ewe would never have made it."

"And those two little lambs would have died, too," Mandy said. "What a good dog you are, Jess!"

She turned to give Jess a hug but Jess was looking away down the hill. Her ears were cocked. She was on the alert.

"What is it, girl?" asked Mandy. "Another ewe in trouble?"

But Jess was off, running down the hill toward the farm, long strides covering the distance fast.

Jenny jumped up and down. "It's Daddy!" she said. "Jess always does that when Daddy comes home."

And Jenny was off after Jess.

"Mrs. Spiller and the baby," Mandy said. "I'd almost forgotten about them."

"Look!" said James.

He was pointing to a tall figure striding up the hill from the farm. Jack Spiller. As they watched, they saw Jess reach him. Mr. Spiller bent down and gave her a pat. Then he saw Jenny running toward him.

Her voice carried on the wind. "Daddy, Daddy, do we have a baby?"

Jack Spiller broke into a run and gathered his daughter up in his arms, lifting her high over his head.

Mandy felt herself smiling as he swung the little girl up on his shoulders and walked toward them, the dog at his heels.

"A boy!" he shouted as he drew near. "A beautiful baby boy, and Maggie is just fine. Exhausted but fine."

Mandy grinned and looked at the twin lambs, now busy suckling. Their white woolly coats had dried in the breeze. They looked as if they were made out of fluffy cotton wool. Their little tails wagged madly as they fed.

"I'll bet the new baby is just as beautiful as you," Mandy said softly to the lambs.

Four

"Home!" said Mandy as the car turned down the road to Animal Ark.

"I'm exhausted," said James.

Dr. Adam laughed. "Lambing is hard work," he said.

Mandy frowned. "Too hard for one person. Too hard for Mr. Spiller all on his own — especially with Jenny to look after while Mrs. Spiller is in the hospital."

Dr. Adam drove through the gate of Animal Ark, past the wooden sign swinging gently in the breeze. Dr. Adam brought the car to a standstill and turned to them. "You know, you could help him," he said. "You were a big help to me today."

Mandy shook her short, fair hair out of her eyes. "Us?" she asked. "But we don't know the first thing about lambing."

"We might do something wrong," said James.

Dr. Adam shrugged. "Just a thought," he said. "But Jack can't be everywhere at once and he certainly can't afford to lose too many lambs. It's a matter of having somebody there to deal with trouble before it happens — like you were doing for me today."

"You mean like Jess and that ewe?" asked James.

Dr. Adam nodded. "That's what I mean. That ewe was ready to bolt. If it hadn't been for you two holding onto her we might have lost the lambs." He smiled. "Think about it," he said.

Mandy's eyes were shining. "We don't have to think about it, do we, James?" she said. "Of course we'll help Mr. Spiller — if he'll let us!"

Dr. Adam laughed. "Oh, I think he'll let you, all right. Jack Spiller has too much on his plate to refuse an offer of help right now."

Mandy smiled up at her dad. He really was kind. If Mr. Spiller needed help, then Mr. Spiller would get help.

"The only thing is . . ." said Dr. Adam.

James and Mandy looked at him. Dr. Adam scratched his ear uncomfortably.

"What is it?" asked Mandy.

"Jack Spiller came here knowing hardly anything about sheep," Dr. Adam said. "And he's done a good job so far — without asking for help."

Mandy began to see what her dad was driving at.

"Oh, Dad, we won't go charging in saying that you've been telling us he's in trouble."

"No, I know you won't," said Dr. Adam. "It's just that he has his pride and he's done a good job already."

"I know," said James. "We'll ask him if he'd train us, sort of — if it wouldn't be too much trouble. How about that?"

"Then we can help him while he thinks he's helping us," said Mandy. "Brilliant! James, you're a genius."

James blushed with pleasure and shoved his glasses up higher on his nose.

Dr. Adam looked at them both. "James might be a genius," he said, "but I'm starving. How about you?"

"Supper," said Mandy. "My stomach feels like a great big empty cave."

"Come on, James," said Dr. Adam. "Call your mom and tell her you're eating with us tonight."

Blackie gave a bark. "And you, too, Blackie." Dr. Adam laughed. "Would I forget you?"

Dr. Emily and Grandma were sitting in the sunny kitchen of Animal Ark. A pot of tea stood on the table between them.

Emily Hope put down her teacup and looked at them in amazement. "Where on earth have you three been?" she asked.

"Have a good picnic?" asked Grandma at the same time.

Mandy looked down at her muddy clothes and even muddier rubber boots. Then she looked at Dr. Adam and James. They weren't any better.

Dr. Adam ran a hand through his hair. "You don't stay clean chasing sheep," he said.

"Sheep?" asked Emily Hope.

"On a picnic?" Grandma said to her son. Adam Hope might be a grown-up vet to the rest of Welford, but to Grandma he was still her boy — and a very muddy one at the moment.

"Tell you what," said Dr. Adam, sidling out of the kitchen. "Why don't we get cleaned up, then we can tell you all about it over supper."

Grandma looked at her watch. "Goodness! Is that the time already?" she said. "I must get home." She bustled about, picking up her coat and giving Emily Hope a hug.

She turned to Mandy and stopped. Mandy grinned. "It's all right, Grandma," she said. "I'm way too muddy to hug. I'll save it for next time."

"Mmm," said Grandma. "Maybe you're right." She put on her coat. "Tell you what," she said. "Stop by tomor-

row, you and James. There's something I want you to
help me with."

"What?" asked Mandy.

Grandma's eyes twinkled. "I'm on the campaigning
trail again," she said.

"Not the post office," said Mandy. "You won that campaign."

Grandma had organized a campaign to save the Mc-
Farlanes' little post office in the village when it was
threatened with closure.

"No," said Grandma. "They're leaving the post office
alone. It's the cottage hospital they want to close now."

Mandy's jaw dropped. "What?" she said. "But they
can't do that!"

Grandma nodded grimly. "They can if they want," she
said. "But I intend to make them change their minds."

"How?" asked Mandy.

Grandma thought for a moment. "I don't know exactly," she admitted. "We'll need a plan. But one thing's
for sure — by the time they're finished, I want them to
regret the day they ever thought of closing the cottage
hospital! So, can I count you in?" She looked from
Mandy to James.

"Of course you can," said James. "I remember getting
my tonsils out there. It's a great place. They gave me ice

cream. And it's so close to school that everybody could come to visit me on their way home. I really liked it."

Mandy thought of the little cottage hospital near their school in Walton. It was as pretty as a picture, with a flower garden in front and green painted shutters on the windows. "What does the head nurse say?" she asked.

Grandma's eyes twinkled even more as she buttoned up her coat. "The head nurse," she said, "is on the warpath."

Mandy felt herself grinning. "Johnny Pearson is terrified of her," she said.

Grandma laughed. "The head nurse's bark is a lot worse than her bite," she said.

"Even when she's on the warpath?" asked James.

Grandma laughed again. "Don't worry, James," she said. "I'm the one you'll be helping." She picked up her bag. "Okay," she said. "I'm off. I'll see you two tomorrow morning."

"Bye, Grandma," Mandy said, and turned to her mother, full of news of Mrs. Spiller's baby and questions about the hospital.

Dr. Emily shook her head. "Oh, no," she said. "Not until you clean yourselves up. Wash first, talk later!"

Mandy, James, and Dr. Adam filed out. Blackie tried to follow them but Dr. Emily stopped him. "Oh, no, you don't," she said. "I'm going to give you a good brushing, Blackie."

Blackie looked resigned. With Emily Hope in this mood it was no good arguing with her.

"That was great," James sighed, leaning back in his chair. "Thanks, Dr. Emily."

Dr. Emily smiled at him. "Glad you enjoyed it, James," she said, looking at the empty plates on the table.

Mandy laughed. "We were hungry, Mom," she said. "Besides, it really was an excellent meal."

They'd eaten quiche and salad and baked potatoes and cheese and coleslaw, followed by the big floury scones Grandma had brought, topped with butter and Dr. Emily's homemade strawberry jam. Mandy felt as if she would never move again — and said so.

Dr. Adam laughed. "And who's going to help your poor old father with the animals tonight?" he asked.

"You know I wouldn't miss that, Dad," Mandy said. "I love helping in the clinic — but maybe not right away."

"I would hope not," said Dr. Emily. "You ate like a horse, Mandy." She looked at her daughter, slim and long-legged. "I honestly don't know where you put it!" she said. She leaned her elbows on the table. "It will really please Grandma if you help her with this campaign."

Mandy looked indignant. "Of course we'll help her. I mean, how can they think of closing the cottage hospital?"

"To save money," Dr. Adam said.

Mandy shook her head. "And what about the people who live here — what about Mrs. Spiller?" she said.

"That's true," said Dr. Emily. "From what your dad says, Mrs. Spiller got to the hospital just in time. That little baby was in quite a hurry to be born."

Adam Hope nodded in agreement. "And there's the visiting," he said. "Jack Spiller would never manage to visit every day if they were much farther away — not at lambing time."

Emily Hope nodded. "That's a good angle to take for your campaign, Mandy," she said. "It isn't just a hospital — it's a lifeline in a place like this."

James grinned. "And that's a good slogan," he said. "'It isn't just a hospital — it's a lifeline.' Do you think your grandma will want to do posters?" he asked.

Mandy laughed. "You know Grandma, she'll want to do everything," she said. "Come on, let's take care of the animals and talk about it."

"Okay," said James, getting up from the table.

"We'll start on the cages, Dad," said Mandy.

"All right," said Dr. Adam. "I'll be there in a few minutes to do the dressings and medications."

"Oh," said Dr. Emily, "that reminds me. Tom is in again. And he isn't too happy about the dressing I put on him this afternoon."

"Tom?" said Mandy. "Again? What happened this time?"

Dr. Emily smiled. "He took on a terrier twice his size — and he got the worst of it. Five stitches. And stitching Tom up is not my favorite job."

Mandy shook her head. Tom was Walter Pickard's big

black-and-white cat. He was a real gangster of the cat world, always in trouble.

"So what's the plan?" asked James as they made their way into the residential unit.

Mandy looked around. There weren't too many animals in at the moment. A puppy with an infected ear, a gerbil with an eye infection, a tortoise with a rather serious cyst, and Tom. Mandy looked at him, crouched like a sleeping lion in his cage.

"I guess we should do a poster campaign. Then maybe a petition."

"And try to get the *Walton Gazette* involved," said James.

"Good idea," Mandy said. "We should even try to get one of the big papers in York interested."

"Steady," Mandy said as James approached Tom's cage. "You undo the latch while I try to charm him out of there."

Tom lifted his great black-and-white head and regarded them lazily. The black patch over one eye made him look like a pirate.

"Okay, Tom," James said to him. "No need to get annoyed. We just want to clean your cage out, that's all."

Tom's massive head swung to look at James and his yellow eyes focused. Then, very slowly, he gathered himself up onto his haunches and hissed.

"Oh, Tom," said Mandy. "We're only trying to help." She looked at the dressing on the back of his neck. It was pretty thickly wadded. He must have gotten a bad bite from that dog. "Oh, Tom," she said again, "why do you get yourself into trouble all the time?"

"That's a question we all ask ourselves," said Dr. Adam, coming into the residential unit. He smiled at Mandy and James. "That cage looks pretty clean to me," he said. "Why don't you leave it until tomorrow? Maybe Tom will be feeling a bit better by then."

Mandy grinned. "You think so?" she asked.

Dr. Adam laughed. "No, I don't," he said. "But you look dead on your feet. It's time you were off to bed. And James's mom will think he's lost."

"I'm pretty tired, too," said James. "An early night isn't a bad idea."

Mandy gave an enormous yawn. Tom opened his huge jaws and did the same.

"Good night, Tom," Mandy said. "Sleep well."

Tom gave her a dismissive look and, turning his back on all of them, curled up and went to sleep.

Five

For the next week Mandy didn't know whether she was coming or going. When they weren't at Lilac Cottage doing posters and leaflets for Grandma, they were at Fordbeck Farm helping Mr. Spiller.

By the end of the week Mandy had designed a dozen posters with the lifeline slogan, and she also felt she knew nearly everything there was to know about lambing. The weather had been really good, and Jack Spiller was pleased with the crop of little lambs. None of the new lambs had to be brought into the kitchen, and the ones that Mrs. Spiller had been hand rearing were almost ready to be put out in the field.

"I really appreciate your help," Mr. Spiller said to Mandy and James as they stood in the top field watching several woolly lambs frolicking around their mothers.

"We haven't done much," said James.

Jack Spiller laughed. "You've done enough," he said. "Keeping an eye out and letting me know at any sign of trouble, catching the ewes when they bolt, bringing the extra feed. Even helping with the hand rearing. It all helps."

Mandy and James blushed with pleasure.

"We've enjoyed it," Mandy said.

"Especially chasing the bolting ewes," James said. "Why do they do that?"

Jack Spiller shook his head. "I think they get frightened," he said. "But one thing is for sure, it's a lot harder to catch a bolting ewe on your own!"

They all laughed. It was a wonderful spring morning. A light breeze stirred Mandy's hair against her cheek. The sky was blue and the sun shone.

"It's a beautiful day for Mrs. Spiller to come home," she said.

Jack Spiller's face split into a wide grin. "It certainly

is," he said. "And I'll be glad to have them back — both of them." His grin got even wider.

"Have you decided what to name the baby?" Mandy asked.

Mr. Spiller looked a bit shy all of a sudden. "We thought Adam," he said. "After your dad. If it hadn't been for him arriving to see if he could help that day . . ." He didn't finish.

Mandy tried to imagine what would have happened if they hadn't stopped by on their way to their picnic. Would Mrs. Spiller have been all right?

"I think that's wonderful," Mandy said. "Dad will be so happy."

Jack Spiller's face look relieved. "You don't think he'll mind?"

"Mind?" said Mandy. "He'll be like a dog with two tails. Just you wait and see."

Jack Spiller grinned again. He looked very young when he wasn't looking worried. "If it had been a girl we'd have named her Mandy," he said.

Mandy felt herself blush. "A boy is nice," she said, embarrassed. "You've got a girl already."

At that, Jack Spiller looked down toward the farmyard, where Jenny was playing with Blackie. "She just loves that dog," he said.

"And Blackie has a great time with her," said James. "She really looks after him well and it means we don't have to tie him up."

Mandy looked at her watch. "Mr. Spiller," she said, "what time did you say you were picking up Mrs. Spiller and the baby?"

Jack Spiller looked at his own watch. "Oh, Lord," he said, "I'll have to run. You're sure you'll be all right while I'm gone?"

Mandy smiled. "Of course we will," she said. "We'll have the kettle on for a cup of tea for Mrs. Spiller when you get back."

They watched as Jack Spiller strode off down the field and into the farmyard. He scooped up his daughter, and they saw him get into the van and start off down the road.

"Adam," Mandy said. "Isn't that nice?"

James grinned. "Come on," he said. "We've got work to do!" And he whistled to Jess to come to heel.

"Over here," Mandy said worriedly.

James came and crouched beside her where she was stationed, keeping an eye on one of the ewes a short distance away.

"What is it?" he asked.

Mandy frowned. "That ewe," she said. "She's had

twins but she only licked one of them. The other one is just lying there."

James looked at her and Mandy felt her heart sink. "No, James. He isn't dead. I'm sure he isn't."

She looked over at the little bundle of wool lying on the short turf, neglected by his mother. He was a tiny black lamb, only minutes old. She had watched him being born.

"So what do we do?" said James.

Mandy shrugged. "Dad said we shouldn't frighten the ewe in a situation like this."

James nodded. "She would only bolt. We can't risk going near her, can we?"

Mandy considered. "Maybe we can," she said. "After all, she's looking after the first lamb."

"Maybe the other one just has to wait his turn," said James.

Mandy shook her head. "I've been watching," she said. "The poor little thing struggled all the way around to his mother's side but she just pushed him away. She's only interested in the first one."

"So what can we do?" asked James.

Mandy looked at him. "You know what Dad said," she said. "If a lamb doesn't bond with the mother right away, then she won't feed it or look after it."

James frowned. "So we have to try to get them together, one way or another," he said. "There isn't anything else to do."

Mandy nodded. "I think you're right," she said. "We have to risk it. But I wish Mr. Spiller or Dad was here."

James looked at his watch. "Mr. Spiller shouldn't be too long," he said. "Do you want to wait?"

But Mandy shook her head. The little black lamb was lying very still now. She didn't want to risk his life. "I don't think we can afford to wait," she said.

"Okay," said James.

"Quietly, James," Mandy said. "We don't want to scare the ewe."

Softly, Mandy whistled for Jess. There was a swift, flowing movement as the black-and-white dog came over the grass toward them, looking at Mandy with intelligent eyes.

"Hold her, Jess," Mandy whispered to Jess.

Jess turned at once and went to the ewe, standing silently at her head, ready to stop her if she should bolt. But the ewe was too busy with the other lamb. She hardly paid any attention to the sheepdog.

Quietly, Mandy and James approached the ewe. Mandy kneeled beside the wet little black bundle on the ground. Gently she lifted the lamb closer to his mother. The lamb stirred in her arms as she did so and Mandy's heart fluttered. He was so small, so delicate.

The ewe paid no attention. Mandy tried everything. She almost pushed the poor little lamb under the ewe's nose but it was no good. The ewe had time for only one lamb, and it wasn't this one.

It was when the ewe raised her head and gave an unmistakably angry bleat that Mandy knew it was useless.

"She's rejected him," said James.

Mandy looked down at the lamb. "Poor little thing," she said. "What should we do?"

James was brisk. "First we get him cleaned up," he said. "Then we try to feed him."

Mandy smiled. "Of course," she said. But she looked down again at the poor little thing. "Poor lamb," she said. "We'll take care of you."

James rummaged in the lambing bag for a rough towel. He handed it to Mandy, and she wrapped it around the lamb, drying him, warming him. Although the day was mild, there was still a stiff breeze, and this little thing was only just born.

As they carried the lamb to the shelter of the drystone wall Mandy looked back. The ewe was looking as proud as could be, suckling her other lamb. Mandy shook her head. Sometimes she just didn't understand nature.

But one thing was sure. They had to get some food into this lamb — and quickly. Carefully she put the lamb inside the lambing bag. It would be cozy there, lying on the fleecy lining. They started down toward the farm.

Mandy had been in many sheep farmers' kitchens at lambing time. It wasn't unusual to see three or four lambs tucked up in cardboard boxes and set close to the stove or the fire for warmth. The Spillers' kitchen was no different. There were three other little lambs being hand reared — Mandy and James were helping with that.

She settled the little lamb on his towel in front of the fire, then took the feeding bottle out of the lambing bag.

"I'll get some milk," James said.

"Not straight from the fridge," Mandy said. "We should warm it a little."

James nodded. "I'll do that," he said. "You stay with the lamb."

Mandy looked at the little creature lying in front of the fire. Even for a newborn lamb he was tiny. It was hard to believe that such a little thing could survive.

Finally James came back with a saucepan of warm milk. Carefully, Mandy poured it into the feeding bottle and screwed on the nipple. Then she sat down on the floor beside the lamb and lifted his little head.

"Here you are," she said gently. "It's milk. You'll like it."

The lamb's eyes flickered. Then his nose twitched. Mandy rubbed the bottle against his lips and the lamb's tongue came out. Then his mouth fastened on the nipple, and he started to suck hungrily.

Mandy raised her face to James. "Look," she said. "He's feeding."

James grinned. "Looks as if he's going to be all right," he said.

Mandy looked at the stumpy little tail beginning to

wag. "He'll need lots of care, though," she said. "He's so small. Smaller than any of the others."

Mandy had just finished feeding the lamb when they heard the sound of an engine.

"That must be the Spillers," said Mandy.

She laid the lamb gently down on the towel and followed James out into the farmyard.

Jenny was out of the van and across the yard like a whirlwind. "We've got a baby!" she cried excitedly.

Mandy looked beyond her to Mrs. Spiller. She was just getting out of the car with a white woolly bundle in her arms.

"It looks like another lamb," James said, and Mandy gave him a nudge.

"Oh, he's beautiful," she said as Maggie Spiller proudly came to show the baby off.

Jack Spiller grinned. "We're going to have our hands full now," he said.

Jenny ran into the house to find Blackie and tell him the news.

Mandy looked at the proud father and mother. "Oh," she said, "you have two new lambs as well."

Jack Spiller's face beamed. "That's good news," he said. "Just as long as they're healthy." He turned to his wife. "I'll just go and get those lambs from the kitchen. They're ready to go out in the field now. And you won't have time for that sort of thing, now that you've got the baby to take care of."

Jenny ran out of the house. "Daddy, Daddy," she called. "We've got a lamb."

Jack Spiller grinned. "We've got boxes full in there," he said. "But I'm just going to put them out. We won't have time to look after them."

Jenny's face looked stricken. "But it's so little, Daddy," she said.

Jack grinned. "They've been there more than a week," he said. "And we have to get rid of them. Your mom has the baby to take care of now."

Mandy looked at Jack Spiller. He didn't understand. Of course he didn't know about the new little lamb.

Jenny looked up at her father. "Get rid of them? Even the little one?" she said. Her face was stricken.

Mandy turned quickly to Jack Spiller, but he was taking his wife's things from the van, helping her into the house.

"All of them," he said.

He'll understand, Mandy thought. *When he sees the lamb he'll understand.*

She looked around to explain to Jenny that her dad had made a mistake. But Jenny was gone.

Six

"We'll find someone to take care of him," Mandy said. "Won't we, James?"

They were standing in the Spillers' kitchen looking at the new lamb. James looked at Mandy's face. For a moment Mandy thought he was going to point out some difficulty. Then he nodded. "Of course we will," he said. "Just give us a day or two."

Jack Spiller shook his head. "I can't ask Maggie to look after lambs just now — not with a new baby in the house. She's been doing enough of that recently. She's going to have her hands full as it is with me out till all hours with the sheep."

Mandy bit her lip. "Today, then," she said. "If we haven't found anyone by this evening . . ." She stopped.

Jack Spiller nodded. "Okay," he said. "I'll give you till tonight. But I don't see how you're going to get anybody to take in a sickly little thing like that. Lambing is bad enough without having to look after anybody else's lambs."

Mandy's mouth set in a determined line. She *would* find somebody to look after the lamb. After all, she had been an orphan, and Adam and Emily Hope had looked after her. Her parents had been killed in a car crash when she was a baby, and the Hopes had taken her in. She was adopted. Not that it felt like that. To her, Adam and Emily Hope were the best parents anyone could have.

"Till tonight," she said to Jack Spiller. "Don't forget — you promised."

Mandy and James got their bikes from the old, run-down shed in the corner of the farmyard where they had left them. Mandy looked around. There was an old stone water trough in the far corner that looked solid enough. But the rest of the place was falling to pieces.

"This place looks ready to fall down," she said.

Mr. Spiller came out of the house and called out to them. "Don't leave your bikes in there. It's dangerous. I don't let anybody go in there."

"Sorry, Mr. Spiller," Mandy said. "We didn't know."

Jack Spiller ran a hand through his hair. "I forgot to mention it," he said. "I've had so much on my mind." He looked at the old, tumbledown shed. "First thing I do after the lambing is over is knock that old shed down."

Mandy smiled. "It won't be long now," she said.

Jack Spiller grinned back. "Nobody ever tells you what things are really like," he said. "Lambing looks easy enough, but it's far from it."

Mandy laughed. "Animals are always a lot of work, Mr. Spiller," she said. "But they're worth it."

Jack Spiller smiled. "You'll make a great vet some day, Mandy, if you set your mind to it."

Mandy blushed with pleasure. "I hope so," she said. "But right now it's finding a home for that little lamb that's worrying me."

A shadow passed over Mr. Spiller's face. "It isn't that I'm being cruel," he said. "But that lamb is a weakling. It would need a lot of attention — feeding every two hours at least — and even then it might not survive. Maggie just hasn't got the time or the energy for it now — and neither do I."

Mandy nodded. "I understand, Mr. Spiller," she said. "But we'll find somebody who has the time and the energy. All we need is a few hours."

Jack Spiller shook his head. "You sound really confident," he said.

James laughed. "We haven't failed yet," he said.

They waved as they pedaled down the path to the main road.

"Who on earth are we going to ask to take in a weakling lamb?" asked James.

Mandy shrugged. "I don't know," she said. She looked hopeful. "You don't think Mom and Dad —"

"No, I don't," James interrupted her. "You know your parents' rules about that."

Mandy sighed. Her parents were very strict about her bringing orphaned animals home. She knew they were right. Unless you said no to all of them you ended up taking all of them in. And then there would be no room for the animals that people brought to Animal Ark.

"It's a vet's practice," Dr. Emily would say to Mandy, "not a zoo."

"What about Walter Pickard?" Mandy said.

James shook his head. "Tom will be going home soon, and a little lamb like that wouldn't be safe around him."

Mandy sighed. "I guess that rules out a whole lot of people," she said. "Most people have a dog or a cat."

"And Mr. Spiller is right about the farmers," said

James. "They're all too busy themselves at the moment to take on a sickly lamb."

"He isn't really sickly," said Mandy. "Just extra small."

James nodded. "So he needs extra feeding — every two hours, right?" he said. "It wouldn't be so bad if he were sick — then we might be able to take him to Animal Ark."

"Or the cottage hospital," said Mandy, laughing. "The head nurse could look after him along with the new babies. I've heard she never gets tired."

Then she stopped talking.

James looked across at her. "What is it?" he asked. "Have you thought of something?"

Mandy turned a shining face to him. "I've had a brilliant idea," she said. "I don't know why I didn't think of it before. We'll take him to Grandma! Grandma and Grandpa can look after him for a week or so — just until he's strong enough to be set on to another ewe."

James's face lit up. "Of course!" he said. "That would be perfect. Your Grandma will love him."

"I hope so," Mandy said. "I have a feeling it's our only chance."

They found Grandpa in the backyard, hoeing his vegetables.

"Hi, Grandpa," Mandy said as they parked the bikes in the back lane.

"Mandy!" said Grandpa, his eyes lighting up with pleasure. "And James. Just give me a minute and I'll make some cocoa."

"No, no," Mandy said quickly. "Let me."

Grandpa's eyes twinkled. "Uh-oh," he said. "Do I see somebody who wants a favor?"

Mandy laughed. "Am I really that bad?" she asked.

Grandpa stuck his hoe in the ground beside him. "You're not bad at all," he said. "It's just that your face gives you away. What is it you want?"

Mandy bit her lip. "I would have to ask both of you," she said. "You and Grandma."

Grandpa shook his head. "Your grandma is off organizing half the village over this hospital closure," he said. "She's called a meeting of the women's club in the church hall." Grandma was chairperson of the Welford Women's Club.

Mandy bit her lip.

"Can it wait?" Grandpa asked.

Mandy looked at James.

"Well," said James, "the sooner we find somebody to take him in the better." Then he stopped.

Grandpa laughed. "I guess the secret is out now," he

said. "Let me try to guess. You're looking for a home for some poor old animal you've found."

"Not old, Grandpa," Mandy said. "Actually he's young — very young."

Grandpa looked seriously at her. "You know we can't take on an animal full-time," he said. "Not the way we are with the trailer home."

Grandma and Grandpa had bought a trailer home when Grandpa retired. They were always taking off on vacations in it. Grandma said it made her feel like an explorer.

Mandy shook her head. "It would only be for a week or so," she said. "Then he will be able to fend for himself — or not exactly fend for himself."

"But he could go out in the top field," said James.

"If we could set him on to another ewe," Mandy finished.

Grandpa looked from one to the other. Then his face cleared.

"You've been up at Fordbeck Farm helping Jack Spiller out," he said.

Mandy nodded. "It's a lamb, Grandpa," she said. "A poor little lamb that has been rejected by his mother. He needs hand rearing for a week or so — just to get him started."

"And we thought you and Mrs. Hope would take him in," said James.

"A lamb?" asked Grandpa.

Mandy looked at him. "Of course," she said. "What did you think it was?"

Grandpa chuckled. "I was beginning to wonder," he said. He pushed his cap to the back of his head and looked at them. "Always up to something, you two," he said. "And there's always an animal in there somewhere."

"Will you do it, Grandpa?" Mandy asked eagerly. "Do you think Grandma will agree? It'll be a lot of work."

Grandpa's eyes twinkled. "Tell you what," he said. "Let's go inside and get the kettle on and cut some of that freshly baked fruitcake. We can have it ready for her when she comes back. Then, when she's had a nice cup of tea, we'll ask her."

Mandy looked at her grandpa in mock outrage. "And you say *I'm* bad?" she said.

Grandpa laughed and tucked her arm into his as they walked down the path to the house. "Can't imagine where you get it from," he said, winking at James.

Seven

Mandy and James hurtled down the road to Fordbeck
Farm, feet pedaling madly, bicycle wheels whizzing.

"It's all right!" Mandy called as they swept into the
yard in front of the farmhouse.

James came to a skidding halt beside her and looked
up at Jack Spiller. "Mandy's grandma and grandpa are
going to take the lamb," he said. "We've found a home
for him. I told you we would."

Jack Spiller didn't smile.

"What's wrong?" Mandy asked.

Suddenly her heart felt heavy as lead. The little animal couldn't have died. He had been weak, yes, but not

so weak as to die in a couple of hours. And Jack Spiller had promised to look after him until they came back.

Mandy stood there watching him as he shook his head.

"I don't understand it," he said. "He was there in front of the fire."

"What do you mean, *was*?" asked James, puzzled.

Jack Spiller spread his hands. "Come and see," he said.

Mandy and James followed him into the kitchen. Mrs. Spiller was sitting in front of the fire, the baby cradled in her arms.

At her feet was a box with a clean piece of wadded sacking in it.

"There," said Jack Spiller. "That's where I left him. And when I came back half an hour later he was gone."

Mrs. Spiller shook her head. "Poor little thing," she said. "It didn't look to me as if he could get very far on his own. Still, it's amazing how tough these hill sheep can be. Maybe the little thing wandered off."

Mr. Spiller looked completely puzzled. "I don't see what else could have happened," he said. "But I would have sworn that little fellow wasn't strong enough."

Mandy was worried. "But if he's run off, what will happen to him? Who will feed him?"

Mr. Spiller shook his head. "Even if he manages to

find his way back to the other sheep, none of them will
feed him," he said.

"But haven't you looked for him?" asked James.

Jack Spiller turned to him, and Mandy saw how tired
he looked.

"There have been a couple of sick ewes up in the top
field," he said. "I've been up there this past hour. But I
didn't see the little fellow."

Mandy turned to Mrs. Spiller. But she shook her head. "I was taking a very welcome nap," she said. "And now I have to feed the baby — if I can find that bottle." She turned to her husband. "Jack, I made up a bottle and put it in the fridge. You haven't seen it, have you?"

Mrs. Spiller stood up and went out of the room with the baby. "I must have left it somewhere," she said. "I'll lose my head next."

Mr. Spiller pursed his mouth. "Look, you two," he said. "I'm really sorry about this. I left that lamb there and now he's gone." He smiled. "At least he was strong enough to get up and go," he said.

Mandy felt troubled. "Maybe he was," she said. "But he can't feed himself, not yet. And none of those other ewes will feed him." She felt tears prick at the back of her eyes and blinked them back as she looked out the window.

It was evening. The sky was darkening. And out on the hill was the little lamb she and James had saved, had found a home for.

"He won't last the night," James said, putting all her fears into words. "Not if he's out there on the hill with no mother to shelter him or feed him."

All of a sudden Mandy made up her mind. "Come on, James," she said. "We'll look for him." She turned to Jack Spiller. "Is that all right with you, Mr. Spiller?"

Jack Spiller looked out the window to where the light was waning. "It'll be dark soon," he said. Then he saw Mandy's face. "But of course you can try. Take a flashlight."

Gratefully, Mandy and James went with him while he looked for a powerful flashlight. Then they were running uphill toward the top field, searching the ditches on the way, looking behind drystone walls and into hedges. And all the time it was getting darker.

Neither of them said how hard it would be to find a tiny black lamb in the dark. Neither of them wanted to think about that. The wind blew cold and Mandy turned her collar up. *Poor little thing*, she thought. They had to find him.

"It's no use," James said at last. "We're only scaring the sheep. And that can't be good for the ones that are still waiting to lamb."

Mandy started to argue, then thought better of it. James was right. For nearly an hour they had searched the field, burrowed in ditches, torn their clothes and hands on thornbushes. And now it was almost dark. But she didn't want to give up.

"Just one more look around, James," she said.

But it was no use. Wearily they trudged downhill — empty-handed.

Jack Spiller met them at the farmyard. He didn't have

to ask. He could see by the look on their faces that they hadn't found the lamb.

"He might not have survived anyway," the farmer said, and Mandy nearly burst into tears.

Oh, yes, he would, she thought. *If he'd had a nice cozy place by the fire at Lilac Cottage and Grandma and Grandpa to fuss over him and look after him —* *he would have survived.*

But it was no good trying to say that to Mr. Spiller. He was only trying to comfort them in his own way. And farmers had to be tough to survive. They couldn't become sentimental about losing lambs. It happened too often.

"Come in and have some milk and cookies before you go," Jack Spiller said. "And tell Maggie and Jenny I'll be right in. I have to go and take a quick look at that old bulldozer in the far field before it gets too dark."

Mandy and James walked into the warm and welcoming front kitchen. Maggie Spiller looked up at them and smiled. The baby was lying asleep in her arms.

"Isn't he beautiful?" said Mandy.

Mrs. Spiller smiled proudly and touched the baby's cheek gently with her fingertip. "He is now," she said. "But he'll probably grow up just as wild as Jenny!" She looked up, still smiling. "Where is Jenny?" she said.

Mandy looked around. "Isn't she here?" she asked.

Maggie Spiller's eyes looked at her sharply. "I thought she had gone with you," she said.

Mandy and James shook their heads. "We haven't seen her," Mandy said.

"But she was here in the kitchen just before you arrived," Mrs. Spiller said. She was looking distraught. Then her face cleared. "Of course! She must be with her dad."

She looked at Mandy and James, and the smile died on her lips.

Mandy bit her lip. "We met him outside, Mrs. Spiller," Mandy said. "He said he was going over to have a look at the old bulldozer. He said we were to tell you and Jenny he wouldn't be long."

Maggie Spiller's face was paper-white. "Me and Jenny?" she said. "But Jenny isn't here. Jenny hasn't been in the house for the last hour or so." Mandy and James looked at her as she sat, her face pale and drawn, holding the new baby close to her.

"Where is Jenny?" Mrs. Spiller said for the second time.

It was at that moment that they heard a crash. It came from outside in the yard. Mrs. Spiller turned toward the sound.

"What was that?" she asked.

Eight

The sound seemed to echo around them. Mandy stood, rooted to the spot, her eyes still fixed on Mrs. Spiller and the baby.

"What was that?" Mrs. Spiller asked again.

Her hand went to her mouth. Then she stood up quickly and tucked the sleeping baby into his bassinet. Her face was grim as she turned to them.

Mandy rushed to the window and looked out. Blackie went with her. He jumped up, resting his front paws on the window ledge. Then he was down again and running out into the yard.

"Blackie!" James called after him. But the Labrador paid no attention.

There was dust still settling in the far corner of the farmyard.

"What is it?" asked James.

"It's the old shed," Mandy said, turning back into the room. "The one Mr. Spiller said was dangerous. It's collapsed."

"That shed," Mrs. Spiller said. "I've been telling Jack. Something needs to be done about it." Her breath caught in her throat. "You don't think . . . not Jenny . . . she can't be . . ." Then she was running for the door and out into the yard.

"Come on," Mandy said to James. "It might still be dangerous!"

They raced out into the yard and stood looking at the far corner where a heap of rubble lay. One side of the shed had collapsed entirely, while the other side looked ready to collapse at any moment. Blackie prowled around the edges of the rubble.

"You don't think Jenny is in there, do you?" James asked.

"Why should she be?" Mandy said. "She was told to keep away from it. Mr. Spiller said nobody was allowed to go near it."

James nodded. "You're right," he said. "But what about Mrs. Spiller?"

Mrs. Spiller was standing by the ruins of the shed. She was calling Jenny's name.

Mandy went to stand beside her.

"It's all right, Mrs. Spiller," Mandy started to say.

"But where is Jenny?" Mrs. Spiller asked. She turned, distraught, looking for her daughter. She was more anxious than ever now.

"Look," said Mandy. "Here comes Mr. Spiller." She pointed toward the far field.

At once Mrs. Spiller began to run toward her husband.

Mandy bit her lip. "The poor Spillers," she said. "They aren't having much luck."

James wasn't listening.

"James?" Mandy said. "What is it?"

James shook his head. "Nothing," he said. "I thought I heard something."

Mandy looked at the ruins of the shed where Blackie was sniffing around. "Blackie," she called. "Here, boy."

The black Labrador paid no attention.

"Call him, James," Mandy said. "The rest of that roof looks as if it's going to go any minute."

James was watching Blackie intently.

"Look, Mandy," he said. "Look at the way Blackie's behaving. Sniffing, searching."

Just then Blackie gave a short, sharp bark and looked toward them. Then he began sniffing at a torn-off sheet of corrugated iron.

"Come out of there, Blackie!" James said.

But the dog stayed firm where he was and barked again.

"What do you think he's found?" Mandy asked.

James licked his lips and looked toward the far field. Jack Spiller had started running now. He was shouting something, but he was still too far away for them to hear what it was. One thing was certain: Jenny wasn't with him.

"Do you think it's Jenny?" Mandy asked.

"It might be," James said. He looked at the sagging remains of the roof. The whole structure groaned, and there was a sharp crack somewhere among the timbers.

"It's going to go any minute," said Mandy. "The whole thing is going to collapse."

Blackie looked at them urgently, pawing the corrugated iron and barking.

Mandy and James looked at the remains of the overhanging roof, then at each other. The roof swayed.

"Come on," said Mandy. "We each take an end and lift. We'll be out of there in no time."

Without giving themselves too much time to think, they scrambled over the collapsed wall into the shed. The roof creaked and groaned.

"Lift," said Mandy as she grasped an end of the corrugated iron sheet.

James lifted. Blackie whimpered and began scrabbling at the edges of the sheet. Nothing happened.

"It's stuck," said James, his face grim with effort.

Mandy nodded. "It's wedged under that," she said, pointing to a big stone that had fallen out of the wall. "You shift the stone. I'll lift a corner of the sheet. We don't even know if Jenny is here."

But, Mandy thought, *where else would she be?* The noise of the shed collapsing would have brought her running to see what had happened. The roof creaked again as James pushed on the stone and rolled it out of the way. Mandy bent and eased the corrugated iron sheet up a little. Then she gasped. A bright red rubber boot lay at an awkward angle under the edge of the sheet.

Her face white, Mandy turned to James.

"I saw," he said.

Then he was bending, straining to lift. Above them the roof swayed dangerously. Blackie whined and barked in warning.

"Again," Mandy said through gritted teeth.

Slowly, the corrugated iron sheet lifted. Mandy felt a sharp edge scrape along her forearm. With an almighty effort they pushed it to one side and looked down.

"Is she . . ." James didn't finish the sentence.

Mandy looked at Jenny. The little girl lay at an odd angle, her head twisted to one side. Blood flowed freely from a gash in her forehead and another in her leg. She looked very pale.

"Maybe we shouldn't move her," Mandy said.

James looked up. Above them the roof beams cracked. A great cloud of dust fell and a stone dislodged itself from the wall, hit Mandy's knee, and rolled, banging, on the corrugated iron. The roof creaked and groaned.

"It's going!" James said urgently. "We have to move her. We can't leave her."

Grimly, Mandy nodded, and together they bent and lifted the little girl's body. She was very light.

As they carried her through the door of the shed into the yard Jack Spiller came racing up, his face a mask of horror.

Grabbing hold of Jenny, he took her from them, then urged Mandy and James in front of him across the yard.

Behind them the crash resounded, louder, longer than before as the remains of the roof fell inward.

Mandy and James stood there covered with dust, looking at the shed. Only one corner was intact now. The rest was hanging precariously in ruins.

"Is she hurt?" Mrs. Spiller came running up, face white with strain.

Mr. Spiller shook his head. "She's bleeding badly," he said. "And she's unconscious. We have to get her to the hospital as soon as possible."

Everything was happening at once. Mandy rushed inside for fresh towels to wrap around Jenny's head and leg. Mrs. Spiller collected the baby in his bassinet. Gently, Mr. Spiller laid Jenny in the back of the van, wrapped in a rug, then jumped in and started to rev up the engine.

Mrs. Spiller leaped into the van beside Jenny, the baby on the floor beside her. She looked at Mandy and James. "If you hadn't got her out . . ." she began.

"Go!" said Mandy as Mr. Spiller revved the engine and put the car in gear. "We'll follow on our bikes."

The van surged off down the driveway.

Mandy and James looked at each other. They were filthy, and Mandy saw a long scratch on James's cheek. She looked at herself. There was a graze on her arm.

"Come on," said James. "Let's go to the hospital. It's better than waiting here for news."

*   *   *

The cottage hospital was warm and welcoming, its lights shining out through the gathering darkness. Mandy and James parked their bikes and ran up the steps into the hall.

A young nurse smiled at them. "You two are a mess," she said. "Have you come to get yourselves patched up?"

Mandy frowned. "No," she said. "It's Jenny. Jenny Spiller. Her mom and dad just brought her in."

The smile disappeared from the nurse's face, and Mandy felt her heart grow chilled.

"She's all right, isn't she?" asked James.

The nurse pursed her lips. "The doctor is with her now," she said. "And the head nurse."

"Head nurse?" Mandy said. If the head nurse was there it must be serious.

"What's happening?" asked James.

The nurse looked as if she wasn't going to tell them, then a voice said from the other end of the corridor, "It's all right, Nurse Williams. I'll deal with this."

Mandy and James looked up as the tall, straight figure of the head nurse came quietly down the corridor. Mandy gulped; Johnny Pearson was right. The head nurse was looking at them with a severe expression. She had neat gray hair and piercing blue eyes. She looked very serious indeed.

"Mr. and Mrs. Spiller told me how you rescued Jenny," she said as she reached them.

"Is she going to be all right?" asked Mandy.

The head nurse pursed her lips. "We'll know very soon," she said. "Jenny has a concussion, and she's lost a lot of blood. She also has a broken leg. She's getting a transfusion at the moment."

"A blood transfusion?" Mandy said, and gulped.

The head nurse's expression softened a little.

"Her parents are in my office with the baby," she said. "I don't think they should be disturbed at the moment. Why don't you go into the waiting room if you want to wait and see how she is?"

Mandy and James nodded. "Yes, we'd like to wait," said Mandy.

The head nurse nodded understandingly. "Of course you would," she said.

The waiting room was tiny. It was brightly painted, and there was a pile of magazines and a box of children's toys in the corner. Mandy didn't feel like reading.

She and James sat there in silence. There didn't seem to be anything to say. It was just a matter of waiting.

Nurse Williams looked in on them after half an hour.

"There you are," she said. "Now, I hope you two aren't worrying too much."

Mandy looked at her hopefully. "Any news?" she asked.

Nurse Williams pursed her lips. "No news is good news," she said. "But it's lucky her mom and dad got her here so quickly. If they'd been much later that little girl would have lost too much blood. As it is, they got that transfusion started just in time."

Mandy's mouth went dry with fright. It was much worse than they'd thought.

"Nurse Williams," said a voice from the door, "I wonder if you would look in on the children's ward. Mary Anne Malloy wants to show you her new pajamas." It was the head nurse, looking disapproving.

Nurse Williams flushed to the roots of her hair. "More new pajamas?" she said. "She must have dozens of them." And she bustled off.

"Little Jenny is going to be fine," the head nurse said firmly. "You are not to worry about her." She looked at Mandy. "I've phoned your grandmother, Mandy. She is going to let your parents and James's know where you are."

"Oh, thank you," Mandy said. "I didn't think."

The head nurse smiled. "I know you're worried," she said, "but that doesn't mean we should worry your parents, too."

"No, ma'am," Mandy said meekly. She felt sorry for young Nurse Williams.

Then she looked at the head nurse. The woman's face softened. She turned in the doorway as she was leaving. "I'll put some antiseptic on those cuts before you go," she said.

"Oh," said Mandy, "it's nothing. They don't hurt."

The head nurse merely smiled. Then she was gone.

"They always say that, don't they?" James said gloomily when the head nurse had gone.

"What?" asked Mandy.

"That people will be fine," James said.

Mandy nodded. "But she will be. I know she will."

At last, there was the sound of voices in the corridor and the whimper of a very young baby crying.

"The Spillers!" Mandy and James said together, and shot out of the waiting room.

Mandy looked at Maggie Spiller. She was crying. Mandy's heart lurched. Then she realized she was smiling as well.

Mrs. Spiller saw Mandy and came over and put her arms around her.

"She's going to be all right, thanks to you two," Mrs. Spiller said. "She needed some blood really quickly, but she'll be okay now."

Mandy smiled up at her, then she looked at Mr. Spiller. But he wasn't smiling. His face was grim.

He came and stood in front of them. "I can't thank you two enough," he said. "But right now I'm going home to get that bulldozer fixed, and as soon as it's fixed I'm going to knock down the rest of that shed."

Mrs. Spiller looked at the baby. "This little one needs feeding," she said. "Jenny is asleep and she isn't to be disturbed tonight. Come on, you two. Put your bikes in the back of the van and we'll take you home."

Mandy and James looked at her gratefully. Suddenly they were both very tired.

"One moment," said the head nurse. She eyed them up and down. "I wanted to put some antiseptic on those cuts."

"Oh, don't bother," James said at once. "They don't hurt at all."

"Anyway, Mom will do it," Mandy said, rolling down her sleeve to hide the graze on her arm.

"Mandy's mom is a vet," James said.

The head nurse smiled thinly. "I should hope you appreciate the difference between people and mere animals," she said.

Mere animals! Mandy thought, outraged. She opened her mouth to protest but the Spillers were leaving.

"What does she mean, 'mere animals'?" she said indignantly to James as he hurried her out the door toward the van.

"Shh!" said James. "She'll hear you."

"I don't care if she does," said Mandy. "Mere animals. Huh! It was Blackie who knew Jenny was under all that rubble. If it hadn't been for Blackie, we wouldn't have been able to rescue Jenny. Mere animals! *Wonderful* animals is more like it!"

Nine

"So that's why I was so late getting home," Mandy finished. "And that's why you won't have that little lamb to look after." She looked around at the faces at the table.

Grandma and Grandpa had come for supper at the Hopes' cottage.

"We'd have been happy to look after the little fellow," said Grandpa, "but I must say we were more worried about you."

"The head nurse didn't go into details when she phoned," Grandma said.

"With all that going on, I don't think getting home late is very important," Emily Hope said, smiling.

Mandy noticed she didn't say anything about the lost lamb. There was no point. A lamb as small as that could never survive on his own.

"Poor Mrs. Spiller," Grandma said. "What a worry for her!"

"Farms can be dangerous places for children," Grandpa said. "Especially children not brought up on a farm."

"Mr. Spiller told Jenny never to go into that shed," Mandy said.

Dr. Adam shook his head. "I'm sure he did," he said. "But I have to say I can't blame him for wanting to bulldoze it as soon as possible." He looked at Mandy. "And as for you and James rushing in there . . ."

Mandy looked guilty. She wished James was still here, but he had gone home. "There was nothing else to do," she said.

Her dad smiled, but she could see the worry behind his eyes. "Of course not," he said. "And it all turned out for the best. I just wish you wouldn't get yourselves into these scrapes."

Mandy bit her lip but didn't say anything. She had tried to make as little as possible of the danger, but Jack Spiller had praised her and James to the skies when he brought them back to Animal Ark.

"Time enough for all that tomorrow," Dr. Emily said. "Mandy, your eyes are almost closed, you're so tired."

Mandy yawned. "What about the animals?" she asked.

"The medications are all done," Dr. Emily said. "Don't worry about that." She looked at her daughter. "I think you should take a bath to ease those bruises, and I'll come up later and put some cream on your cuts."

Mandy made a face. "The head nurse wanted to put antiseptic on them," she said.

Mom laughed. "I'll bet she did," she said. "Don't worry, this cream won't sting."

Mandy yawned again as she got up from the table.

"Good night, Grandma," she said, but Grandma didn't answer. She was staring into space.

"Grandma?" Mandy said.

"Oh, yes, sorry," Grandma said. "I was miles away."

Grandpa laughed. "Maybe you need an early night as well," he said.

But Grandma was as bright as a button. "No," she said. "It's just that something occurred to me." She turned to Mandy. "You said that the head nurse told you Jenny got her blood transfusion just in time?" she asked.

Mandy shook her head. "It wasn't the head nurse, it was Nurse Williams who said that."

Grandma nodded. "That sounds more like it," she said. "The head nurse would be far too discreet to say a thing like that."

"What are you getting at?" asked Grandpa.

Grandma turned to him. "I was wondering what would have happened if Jenny hadn't been able to have that blood transfusion when she did."

Mandy shivered. "But she did, Grandma. That's all that matters," she said.

Grandpa laid a hand on Grandma's arm. "I know you feel really sorry for the Spillers and the trouble they've had lately, but the little girl is getting better now."

"Only because she got that blood transfusion," said Grandma.

Grandpa looked puzzled. "Of course," he said.

"But don't you see?" said Grandma. "If Jenny hadn't gotten that transfusion so quickly she might have died. What I'm getting at is, if the accident had happened after they closed the cottage hospital, Jenny wouldn't have gotten that transfusion so quickly. What happens if there is another accident like this — after the hospital is closed?"

Mandy looked at her. "Of course," she said. "I didn't think of that."

Grandma nodded. Her face was very serious. "As your Grandpa says, farms can be dangerous places, and accidents can easily happen." She looked around the table. "We need that hospital," she said. "It really is a lifeline for us. And I'm going to make sure that we keep it."

Mandy threw her arms around Grandma's neck and hugged her. "And I'll help you," she said. "What do you want me to do?"

Grandma squeezed Mandy's hands. "Tomorrow I'll go and see Marion Timpson," she said.

"Who?" asked Mandy.

Grandma's eyes twinkled. "The head nurse," she said. "She isn't happy about this closure business. In fact, she's hopping mad about it."

Mandy blinked. She couldn't imagine the frosty head nurse hopping mad about anything.

"The campaign is all very well as it is," Grandma said, "but we aren't making an impression on people. We have to get the message across. That hospital is important. It isn't like other things. Keeping it open could make the difference between life and death. And if it takes a fight to keep it open, then I'll fight. And so will a whole lot of other people in Welford and Walton."

Grandma paused, then her eyes lit up. "In fact," she went on, "if they're trying to close one cottage hospital, you can bet your boots they're trying to close others. I wouldn't be surprised if there are a whole lot of communities facing this at the moment." Her head came up. "What we need," she said, "is a national campaign. We need to get the media on to this. Press coverage, TV. You wait and see. Once I'm finished we'll have a whole lot of support from all over the country, you see if we don't. Close our cottage hospital? Over my dead body!" Grandma finished triumphantly.

Mandy gave Grandma an extra hug. Adam Hope began to clap, and Emily Hope and Grandpa joined in.

"What a speech!" Dr. Adam said. "One thing's for sure, we're all behind you."

"Just let us know," Dr. Emily said. "Fund-raising, posters, you name it — we'll help."

Grandpa didn't say anything. Mandy looked at him, puzzled. Then she saw the pride in his eyes as he looked at his feisty wife. "Come on, Dorothy," he said to Grandma. "Time we were off." He turned to Dr. Emily. "I'll take this firebrand out of your kitchen, Emily, before she sets the whole place ablaze!"

Emily Hope laughed. "You don't fool us," she said. "You're proud of your firebrand. And she can set our kitchen ablaze any time she likes."

"Ouch!" said Mandy as she emerged from sleep next morning. She looked around her, puzzled for a moment. Why did she feel stiff and sore? Then she remembered the events of the day before and sighed in relief. Jenny was all right. She and James were going to the hospital today to check up on her.

It took a moment before Mandy remembered the little black lamb. Her mouth turned down. There was no way the little fellow could have survived a night outside with no mother to protect him. Mandy would just have to put him out of her mind. There was nothing else to do.

Mandy threw back her comforter and swung her legs out of bed. She winced again. There was an ugly looking bruise on her knee.

"At least the head nurse won't see it," she said to herself as she crossed the room toward the window.

Leaning across the pine table at the window, Mandy drew the flowery curtain aside and looked down into the garden.

A whole family of rabbits scuttled around, tearing up mouthfuls of grass, chasing one another in and out of bushes. Mandy laughed at their antics and turned back to her room. With its old pine furniture and posters of animals it was her haven.

"Mandy," a voice called from downstairs.

Mandy threw open her bedroom door and leaned over the banister to look down the twisty stairs. "Good morning," she called back to her mother.

"James just called," her mom called back. "He'll be over in half an hour."

"Good," said Mandy. "We're going to the hospital to see Jenny."

"You might see Grandma," Dr. Emily called back. "She's going over to see the head nurse this morning. She's bursting with energy over this campaign. Scrambled eggs for breakfast?"

Mandy laughed at the change of subject. "Yummy!" she said. "I'll be there in five minutes."

A quick shower, a clean shirt, and a fresh pair of jeans and Mandy was running downstairs, her hair still damp.

Dr. Adam emerged from the door that led to the clinic. "You did the morning medications," Mandy said. "Did I oversleep?"

Her dad grinned and ruffled her hair. "Don't you think you deserved an extra half hour after yesterday?" he said.

Mandy frowned. "I like helping you," she said.

"I know you do," said Dr. Adam. "And you can give your mom a hand with the evening medications. I'm going to be out late doing tuberculin injections."

"Hard work," Mandy said. "But worth it." She knew the injections helped to stop cows from passing on tuberculosis. "How is Tom?"

Dr. Adam grinned. "Back to his old antisocial ways.

Honestly, they might talk about a cat having nine lives, but that animal has twice that at least."

"I'll just stop by and see him before breakfast," Mandy said.

A bright red head peeked around the door. "Oh, no, you won't," said Emily Hope. "Breakfast is on the table. You can go and see Tom afterward — and add a few scratches to the ones you've already got." She looked worriedly at her daughter, then her face cleared. "You look completely recovered," she said.

Mandy grinned. "Oh, I'm fine," she said. "But I'm starving."

Dr. Emily laughed. "That's a good sign at least," she said. "Come on, before the eggs get cold."

Mandy followed her mom into the kitchen. The sun shone through the windows, making the copper pans sparkle where they hung on the oak beams. The table was set with a fresh, red-checked cloth, and on it stood a plate of honey-colored toast, a dish of pancakes, and a huge mound of butter-yellow scrambled eggs in a blue bowl.

"Terrific!" Mandy said with feeling.

Mandy was just polishing off the last pancake when she heard the sound of a bike scattering the gravel in the driveway.

"It's James," said Dr. Emily, looking out the window. "And Blackie."

"I'm off," said Dr. Adam. "And don't you two get into any mischief today. Your mom and I have had enough excitement for one week."

Mandy grinned. "Don't worry," she said. "James and I have had enough, too."

"Enough what?" said a voice, and James appeared around the kitchen door, brushing his brown, floppy hair out of his eyes.

"Excitement," said Mandy.

"Right," James said. "I had to promise Mom I would behave before she let me out. Behave? We didn't do anything wrong."

Dr. Adam laughed as he gathered up his vet's bag and passed James on the way to the door. "Parents always blame you when they're worried about you," he said. "You just have to put up with it."

James grinned back. "I guess so," he said. His eyes went to the table. "Did you have pancakes?" he asked.

Emily Hope looked at Mandy and James and shook her head. "I don't know where you two put all the food you eat," she said. "There isn't an ounce of fat on either of you."

"I'm going to go now," Dr. Adam said, sidling out of the door.

Mandy laughed. Dr. Emily was always nagging him about his weight. It wasn't that he was fat — just not thin. And he did jog to try to keep his weight down.

"Bye, Dad," she called after him.

Dr. Emily looked at her watch.

"Surgery in half an hour," she said. "Tell you what. You two go and look in on Tom, and I'll make another batch of pancakes. I'll call you when they're ready."

"Great," said James. "You make the best pancakes, Dr. Emily."

Dr. Emily grinned. "Flattery will get you everywhere, James," she said. She looked at Blackie. "I guess you want some, too?" she said.

Blackie wagged his tail, and Mandy just managed to catch the butter dish before it was swept off the table.

Tom was, as Dr. Adam had said, getting better.

"Ow!" said James as he lifted the cat out of the cage.

"His claws are really sharp," Mandy said.

James sucked his hand. "I know," he said. "What a monster!"

Mandy looked at the old cat. "He isn't a monster," she said. "Just a little grumpy."

"Grumpy is pretty normal for Tom," James said.

Mandy frowned. "I hope Jenny is back to normal today," she said. "Poor little girl. She must have gotten a terrible shock."

James put Tom back in his cage. "Let's go this morning," he said. "As soon as we've had the pancakes. The head nurse has to let us see her today."

Mandy nodded. Jenny had to be well enough to have visitors today.

Dr. Emily called them back just as they were leaving. "Take this to Jenny," she said, holding out a prettily wrapped package.

"Thanks, Mom," said Mandy. "What is it?"

"Soaps," said Dr. Emily, "shaped like flowers. I thought she would like them."

"She will," said Mandy.

"Mom sent some fruit," said James.

"And I have a card and a little game here for her," Jean Knox said. "Just hold on while I write out the card."

Mandy looked at the receptionist with affection as Jean caught the glasses swinging from their chain around her neck, put them on, and wrote a message on the card.

"Thanks, Jean," she said. "It'll be like Christmas."

James called to Blackie and they were off down the road from Animal Ark, heading for Walton Road.

They passed Walter Pickard on his way to the church for bell-ringing practice. He was carrying a big bunch of flowers from his garden. "Your grandpa tells me you've been getting yourself into some mischief lately, young lady," he called to Mandy.

Mandy grinned and stopped her bike. "So has Tom," she said.

Walter scratched his head. "You'd think he'd be old enough to know better, wouldn't you?" he said. "Your mom says I can have him back tomorrow — if I can keep him out of trouble."

Mandy laughed at the idea of keeping Tom out of trouble.

"We've been told to stay out of trouble, too," James said gloomily.

Walter laughed. "Where are you two young ones off to?"

"The cottage hospital," Mandy said. "To see Jenny Spiller."

Walter grinned. "At least you can't get into any trouble in a hospital," he said. Then he shook his head. "Bad business, that," he said. "But you two did well from what I hear. You tell the little lass I'm asking for her," he went on. He looked at the flowers he was carrying. "I was taking these along to the church for the Women's

Club to arrange," he said. "But I reckon young Jenny would like them. Here you are, young miss," and he handed the bunch of flowers to Mandy.

"Oh, Mr. Pickard, thank you," Mandy said as she put the flowers in her bicycle basket. "They're beautiful. Jenny will be so happy."

Julian Hardy, who owned the Fox and Goose, stepped out of his pub when he saw them coming. "How's little Jenny?" he asked.

Mandy smiled. News certainly got around fast in Welford. "We're going to see her now," she said.

"Wait there, then," Mr. Hardy said, and disappeared into the pub. He was out again in a moment carrying a bottle of orange soda. "Give her this from me," he said.

It was like that all through the village. Mrs. McFarlane from the post office saw them passing and called them in while she made up a pile of comics to take to Jenny. By the time they got to the hospital their bicycle baskets were full of presents. Mandy looked at Blackie trotting along beside them. She smiled. She had the feeling that Blackie might be the best present of all. Jenny liked him so much.

"And Mr. Spiller thought they might not be accepted around here," Mandy said to James.

"What?" said James.

Mandy explained as they rode along. "One of the reasons they kept to themselves was that he thought people would think of them as not really country folk. You know, with him losing his job in the town and all. He thought he might be resented."

Mandy looked at the pile of gifts in her bicycle basket.

"Well," she said, "they can't really think that people don't care about them now!"

Ten

"Where do you think you're going with that dog?" said a voice.

Mandy and James turned.

It was the head nurse, looking really forbidding.

"What does she mean 'that dog'?" James whispered to Mandy. "Blackie isn't 'that dog.'"

"Shh," said Mandy. "She'll hear you."

"I certainly did hear you, James Hunter," said the head nurse as she strode down the corridor toward them.

"We brought Blackie to see Jenny," Mandy said.

"Yes," said James. "She and Blackie get along really well."

The head nurse stopped in front of them and folded her arms. "No animals are allowed inside the hospital," she said.

"But why not?" said Mandy.

The head nurse looked shocked. "Why not?" she said. "Because they're unhygienic, that's why not! They'd bring all kinds of nasty germs into the hospital. We've got sick people here, you know."

Mandy frowned. "We wouldn't let him jump on the beds or anything," she said. "And besides, sick people are supposed to get better quicker if they have pets."

"That's right," James said. "I read that somewhere. Pets are good for sick people."

The head nurse drew herself up. "Not in this hospital," she said. She looked at Mandy. "I was having a long talk with your grandmother this morning about trying to save the hospital," she said. "Your grandmother said you were helping her."

Mandy nodded. "James is helping, too," she said. "We made lots of posters and leaflets and things."

The head nurse sniffed. "Fine way to help," she said, "bringing animals into the hospital. That's just the kind of thing that would do us a lot of harm. If we're going to

run a campaign to save the hospital we have to be sure everything is run perfectly. We can't have animals running around everywhere. Now put that dog outside — and wash your hands before you go into the ward." And the head nurse stomped off down the corridor.

"Huh!" said James. "You'd think we'd brought in a whole zoo full of animals instead of one harmless dog."

Blackie looked up at them with mournful eyes.

"Don't pay any attention to her, Blackie," Mandy said. "We don't think you're full of germs."

They took Blackie outside and left him tied to a tree in the garden before they went back into the hospital to find Jenny.

"Don't stay long," said Nurse Williams.

Mandy and James looked at her.

"She *is* better, isn't she?" Mandy asked.

The nurse smiled. "She's still very tired," she said. "But her broken leg should heal well. It isn't like poor Johnny Pearson's. That was a really bad break." She frowned. "I think something is worrying her, though, but she won't say what it is." Then she looked at the pile of presents Mandy and James were carrying. "I should imagine those will cheer her up," she said.

"Have Mr. and Mrs. Spiller been in today?" Mandy asked.

The nurse nodded. "They were here first thing," she

said. "Isn't that baby a darling? They left a little while ago. Mr. Spiller said he had to get back." The nurse smiled. "Funny man — he said he had a little bulldozing to do."

Mandy frowned as they followed the nurse down the corridor. What could be worrying Jenny?

"You go ahead," said Nurse Williams as she showed them into the bright, sunny ward. She took the bunch of flowers Mandy was carrying. "Aren't these lovely?" she said. "I'll just put them in water." And she walked briskly back down the corridor.

The children's ward was small — only six beds, and three of them were occupied.

Poor Johnny had his leg in traction. His curly red head turned as they came in and he gave them an impish grin. Mandy and James grinned back.

"How are you, Johnny?" Mandy said as they passed his bed.

"Bored," said Johnny. "There's nothing to do."

"You could read," said Mandy.

"I've read all my comics twice," Johnny said. His eyes fell on the bundle of things in Mandy's hands. "Is that this week's comics?" he said.

Mandy nodded, grinning. "Maybe Jenny will let you read them when she's finished with them," she said.

Johnny looked at Jenny over the sling his leg was

caught up in. "I bet she won't even read them," he said. "She just lies there and cries."

Mandy opened her mouth to say something but a voice piped up from the next bed.

"There's somebody she wants to see but when you ask her who it is she won't tell you."

Mandy looked at the next bed. A plump little fair-haired girl was perched on the end of it, brushing the hair of a fair-haired doll. Mandy didn't recognize her.

"Hi," she said. "I'm Mary Anne Malloy. I had my appendix out. I saw it. They showed it to me after the operation. It was disgusting!"

Mandy blinked and heard James laugh beside her.

"You didn't want to take it home in a jar or anything?" he asked.

Mary Anne kept on brushing her doll's hair. The doll had pink pajamas on, just like Mary Anne's.

"No way," she said. She looked up at them. "I wish Jenny felt a bit better. I offered to let her play with Gilda," she held up the doll, "but she didn't want to." Mary Anne sighed.

"That was nice of you," said Mandy. "But maybe she isn't well enough yet."

Mary Anne smiled. "That's probably it," she said. "I felt awful for the first couple of days after I had my appendix out. I was an emergency case."

"With an ambulance and everything?" James asked.

Mary Anne nodded proudly. "Daddy says they stopped all the traffic on Walton Road." She gave them a huge smile. "Imagine that," she said.

Mandy couldn't help laughing. "Imagine," she said. "Look, Mary Anne, we're going to see Jenny now."

"Tell her she can play with Gilda any time she wants," said Mary Anne.

"We will," said Mandy.

"She's a riot," James said as they made their way across to Jenny's bed. It was next to the French windows that opened up into the garden at the back of the cottage hospital. The sun came streaming through the light, flowered curtains onto the neat bed where Jenny lay. Her face was turned away from them.

"Maybe she's asleep," said Mandy.

But at the sound of her voice the head on the pillow turned and Jenny gave them a weak smile.

"Hello," said Mandy. "We brought you some presents. Everybody is asking about you."

Jenny didn't say anything.

James looked uncomfortable. "Is there anything you want?" he said. "Anything we can do for you?"

Jenny shook her head and a big, fat tear ran down her cheek. She moved her lips and said something but so low that they couldn't hear what it was.

"What?" said Mandy.

Jenny turned to her. "Blackie," she said.

Mandy bit her lip. "We brought him," she said. "But the head nurse wouldn't let us bring him in. She won't allow animals into the hospital."

Jenny's face had brightened but now with Mandy's last words she looked sad again.

"He's dead, isn't he?" she said.

Mandy was shocked. "Dead?" she said. "Of course he isn't dead. He's outside, tied to a tree."

Jenny shook her head. "You're just saying that," she said, and another big tear ran down her cheek.

Mandy and James looked at each other as Jenny turned her face away.

"Why on earth does she think he's dead?" asked James.

Mandy shrugged. "I don't know," she said. "But she's obviously worried about it. She won't get better if she goes on worrying like this."

"But we can't bring Blackie in," said James. "You heard the head nurse. She'd kill us."

Mandy nodded, trying to think. Her eyes rested on the French windows beside Jenny's bed.

"We don't have to bring him in," she said. "We just have to bring him around to the windows. Then Jenny can see he isn't dead."

"Brilliant," said James. "You wait here with Jenny. I'll go and get Blackie."

Mandy nodded and James went quickly out of the ward.

"James went to get Blackie," Mandy said to the little girl. "You wait and see. He'll be here in a minute."

Jenny's eyes looked bright with tears. "Are you sure?" she said.

Mandy nodded. "I promise," she said.

There was a tap on the French windows. Mandy went over and unlatched them.

"Look, Jenny," she said. "Blackie's here to see you."

Eagerly the little girl sat up in bed and leaned forward to see. Then her face crumpled. Her mouth dropped, and she said, "Not that Blackie. I want *my* Blackie."

Mandy looked at her in astonishment.

"Your Blackie?" she said. "What do you mean?"

Jenny shook her head, the tears running down her cheeks. "My Blackie," she repeated. "My little black lamb."

Light began to dawn on Mandy.

"What's going on?" said James from beyond the window. "Is she happy?"

Mandy shook her head. "There's a problem," she said. "We've got the wrong Blackie."

"What?" said James. In his surprise he stepped over the sill into the ward. Blackie came with him.

"Oh!" said Mary Anne from her bed. "What a pretty dog. Can I pet him?"

James nodded absently and Mary Anne trotted over to pet Blackie.

Mandy turned to Jenny. "Your lamb," she said. "Is that the one that was missing, the one we left in the kitchen? The tiny one?"

Jenny nodded. "Daddy said we couldn't have it. He said it was too much trouble — it would have to go." She looked up, her little face fixed. "I took him away," she said. "I hid him. Then I took one of the baby's bottles and some milk to feed him — just the way Mom did with those other lambs. I know how. Mom showed me."

James started to speak but Mandy shook her head. Very gently she sat down on Jenny's bed and put her arm around her.

"Jenny," she said, "where did you hide the lamb?"

Jenny's eyes filled with tears again. "If I tell you, then Daddy will get rid of him," she said.

Mandy hesitated. There was no easy way of putting this. "But Jenny," she said, "if your Blackie is all alone, he'll get sick. Lambs as small as that need someone to take care of them."

Again Jenny shook her head. "Daddy would be angry," she said.

Mandy sighed. "But how can we find Blackie and bring him to see you if we don't know where he is?'

Jenny looked up at her. "You wouldn't tell anybody?" she said. "You would bring him here so that I could see he was all right?

"Cross my heart," said Mandy. "And I'll take care of him until you get out of the hospital. I promise."

Jenny looked at her again. "I put him in the shed. The old one."

It took a moment for Mandy to realize what the little girl was saying.

"The old shed?" she said. "The one you got hurt in?"

Jenny looked puzzled and Mandy realized she didn't remember how she got hurt. She had been unconscious when they found her.

"You mean the one your dad told you not to go into? The run-down shed. That one?"

Jenny nodded. "He wouldn't let anybody go in there so I knew nobody would find Blackie."

Mandy and James looked at each other. "Where did you put him?" Mandy said.

Jenny frowned. "Right at the back," she said. "In the water trough, so that he couldn't run away and get hurt."

Mandy conjured up a mental picture of the shed as she had last seen it. The water trough was at the back. As far as she could remember the roof was still intact at that point.

It was then that James said, "The bulldozing — remember what Nurse Williams said?"

Mandy turned to him.

"Oh, no," she said.

"What is it?" asked Jenny.

Quickly Mandy smiled. She couldn't really tell the little girl that her father was going to bulldoze the shed that afternoon.

"It's nothing," Mandy said. "But we have to go." She looked at James.

"We have to go and get your Blackie," James said to Jenny.

Jenny's face lit up. "And bring him back."

"If he's well enough," Mandy said. "You just get better now, okay?"

Jenny smiled and snuggled down in bed. "And don't let Daddy put him out in the field, okay?" she said.

Mandy shook her head. "He won't do that," she said. She turned to James. "We'd better call — just in case."

"I don't believe my eyes!" a voice said — a familiar voice.

Mandy and James turned. The head nurse stood at

the door of the ward. "How dare you disobey my orders?" she said.

"We didn't," said James. Then he looked at where Mary Anne was playing with Blackie. "Uh-oh," he said.

"We have to make a phone call," Mandy said.

The head nurse looked outraged. "Phone call!" she said. "I've never heard such rudeness in my life. Phone call, indeed. You will put that animal outside, then you will report to me in my office." And she turned on her heel and left the ward.

The head nurse was obviously not used to being disobeyed.

Mandy looked at James in horror.

"We have to get in touch with the Spillers," James said.

"She won't let us. She won't listen," said Mandy. "You heard her. She's on the warpath."

"So what do we do?" asked James.

Mandy shrugged. "There's only one thing to do," she said. "We make a run for it. We've got to get to Fordbeck Farm before Mr. Spiller bulldozes that shed!"

Eleven

Mandy's legs were aching by the time the track to Fordbeck Farm came into view.

"What's that noise?" she said as they rounded the bend in the road, earth spurting beneath their wheels.

"Look!" shouted James as he hurtled down the road toward the farm. Mandy followed his gaze.

"Oh, no!" she gasped. "Hurry!"

Jack Spiller was driving the bulldozer through the gate at the back of the farm into the farmyard. He was heading straight for the shed.

"Too late!" James yelled over the increasing roar of the bulldozer.

Mandy thought of Jenny. "We can't be too late," she said.

Together they ran through the farm gates right in front of the bulldozer.

"Stop," they yelled. "Stop!"

Mandy saw Jack Spiller's face look down at them, astonished. He swerved the bulldozer to one side, put on the brakes, and leaped down from the cab.

"What the devil do you two think you're doing?" he yelled. "Do you have any idea how dangerous that was?"

Mandy jumped off her bike and ran to him. "Mr. Spiller," she said. "You have to listen. It's Jenny."

At once Jack Spiller stopped shouting. His face went white. "Jenny?" he said. "Is she all right? What happened?"

Mandy shook her head. "Nothing," she said. "But she's so unhappy because of the lamb — the one that disappeared. Jenny took him — she hid him in the shed. He's still there."

"Say all that again slowly," said Jack Spiller.

Mandy did, with James's help. Blackie arrived, panting, as they finished talking.

"So you see," Mandy finished, "she's so worried about that little lamb, she isn't getting better. We promised her that we'd bring the lamb to see her. He's in that shed,

Mr. Spiller. We told Jenny we'd take care of him — and we will, if he's still alive."

Jack Spiller looked undecided. "That place is dangerous," he said.

Mandy nodded. "I know," she said. "But the lamb is hidden in the old water trough."

"At the back of the shed?" Mr. Spiller asked.

"Yes, the roof hasn't fallen in back there," said James.

Mandy watched as Mr. Spiller weighed the chances of finding the lamb alive.

"It's just that she wanted that little lamb so much," said Mandy.

Jack Spiller made up his mind. "Wait here," he said. "And don't move."

Mandy, James, and Blackie stood watching as Mr. Spiller moved cautiously around to the back of the shed. Part of the wall had given way. They saw him step carefully over the rubble. As he did, his foot scraped on stone and Mandy thought she heard the wall creak. She held her breath. It seemed like ages before he came out again. Mandy looked. Was he carrying something? Yes — something black and woolly.

She looked at Mr. Spiller's face. He was smiling. "He's alive?" she asked.

Jack Spiller shook his head in wonder. "I wouldn't have given a dime for this little thing when I first saw him," he said. "But he's alive, all right. He must be a real fighter. And look at this."

Mandy looked at what he was holding.

"A baby's bottle," she said.

Jack Spiller grinned. "I guess we've found the one that Maggie lost," he said. "Take this little guy into her and see if you can get some fresh milk into him. He was licking the nipple of this bottle when I found him in the water trough. Lucky for him he was there with the bottle beside him. He was protected from the worst of the damage."

"Oh!" said Mandy, taking the little creature. "He's so weak."

Mr. Spiller scratched his head. "I think he'll survive," he said. "After what he's been through I wouldn't put anything past him."

James grinned. "This is going to make Jenny get better fast," he said.

Mr. Spiller grinned back. "In that case I'd better get that shed knocked down," he said. "Before she gets back and starts hiding more animals in there."

Mandy and James took the lamb into the house.

"Good heavens!" said Maggie Spiller when she saw what they were carrying.

Once more Mandy explained, while Mrs. Spiller got some milk ready for the lamb.

"If you have any protein supplement . . ." Mandy began.

Mrs. Spiller nodded. "Your dad left some with us the other day," she said. "I'll get it."

Mandy and James watched as Mrs. Spiller mixed the protein supplement with the milk. Then she handed the bottle to Mandy.

"Here," she said. "See how much of this he'll take."

The lamb was hungry. He sucked eagerly at the mixture in the baby's bottle and after a while his little tail began to wag.

"I really think he's going to be all right," said Mandy.

Mrs. Spiller laughed. "Who would have thought it?" she said. "Our Jenny will be happy."

Mandy smiled. Yes, Jenny would be happy.

"But I want to see him!" Jenny said.

"Just as soon as you get out of the hospital," Mandy said to her.

It was the day after the bulldozing of the shed, and they were visiting Jenny.

Jenny shook her head. "You're only saying he's okay so I won't worry," she said.

"No, we're not," James said. "He's fine, really. Your mom is feeding him and he's amazingly strong. Soon he'll be able to be set on to another ewe."

Jenny looked mutinous. "You're just saying that," she said again.

"Here comes the head nurse," Mary Anne said from the door where she was keeping lookout. Mandy and James had sneaked past her office. She hadn't seen them come in.

"Quick," said James. "We'll go out the windows."

Jenny clutched Mandy's arm. "When will you bring Blackie?" she asked.

"Hurry!" said Mary Anne.

Mandy looked at the little girl desperately. "You know the head nurse won't let animals in the hospital," she said.

"Run!" Mary Anne called.

Jenny looked at Mandy.

"Tomorrow!" Mandy said, then she leaped for the French windows.

Any moment she expected to hear a shout behind her, but there was nothing.

"That was close," said James as they made their way around to the front of the hospital. "How on earth are we going to get the lamb in to see Jenny?"

Mandy shrugged. "Through the French windows, I guess," she said.

James looked doubtful. "We were lucky that time," he said. "But I don't like trying to escape the head nurse's eagle eye very often. And what about Nurse Williams? She's always around."

"We'll manage," said Mandy. "It's obvious Jenny isn't going to get better until she's seen that lamb."

James nodded. "At least you sound confident," he said. "It's more than I feel."

But Mandy didn't feel half as confident as she sounded.

Her confidence didn't improve when she got home, either.

"Grandma called," Dr. Emily said to her.

"Yes," said Mandy.

"She wanted to know what you've been doing to upset the head nurse," Dr. Emily said.

"What?" said Mandy. "What did Grandma say exactly?"

"So you *have* been up to something!" Dr. Emily said.

Mandy sighed. "Not exactly," she said. "It was a mistake."

"Hmm," said Dr. Emily. "I guess I should leave well enough alone and not ask difficult questions," she said.

Mandy looked at her mom gratefully. Dr. Emily knew that if Mandy was in real trouble she would tell her.

"Anyway," Dr. Emily went on, "Grandma says she has a TV crew coming tomorrow to cover the story about the hospital closure. So the head nurse will have other things on her mind." Dr. Emily grinned. "She said to let you know you could relax tomorrow, at least, but the head nurse still wants to see you and James."

Mandy sighed. Life was just too complicated sometimes.

"But we promised to take the lamb to see Jenny tomorrow," James said when she told him.

Mandy nodded. "I know," she said. "But how can we? If the TV crew is going to be there..." Then she stopped.

"What is it?" asked James.

"That's just it," said Mandy. "The TV crew is going to be there. If we find out when they're coming, then we can make sure the head nurse will be busy with them."

"So we take the chance to sneak Jenny's lamb into the ward," James said.

Mandy nodded. "I know we aren't supposed to," she said. "But the head nurse would never listen and Jenny will keep crying until she sees her lamb."

"We'll just have to go for it," said James. "We don't have a choice."

Mandy nodded in agreement.

"So how are we going to find out when the TV crew is coming?" James said.

Mandy frowned. "I'll ask Grandma. She'll be there for the taping. After all, she is the one who organized it."

"Right," said James. "You go and see your grandma, and I'll go up to Fordbeck Farm to see if the lamb is going to be strong enough to take tomorrow."

Mandy nodded. "Okay," she said. "Let's meet at Animal Ark after supper!"

"Eleven o'clock," Mandy said as she and James did the rounds of the animal cages in the residential unit. "First they want an interview with Grandma and the head nurse, then they want to film the wards and talk to the patients."

James grinned. "Can you imagine how happy Mary Anne will be?" he asked. "Does she know?"

Mandy laughed. "Of course she knows," she said. "Can you imagine trying to keep anything secret from Mary Anne? She was supposed to go home this morning but she asked if she could stay just one more day."

"And the head nurse let her?" said James.

Mandy grinned. "Grandma pointed out to the head nurse that the more patients they had, the better it would look."

"Your grandma is amazing," James said.

"Grandma also says that Mary Anne's mother brought

her another new nightgown and a matching one for Gilda."

James shook his head. "She'll be a riot on TV," he said.

"Who? Grandma or Mary Anne?" asked Mandy.

"Both!" James said.

"What about Blackie?" Mandy asked.

"I don't think we'll take him," said James. "That's asking for trouble."

"Not your Blackie, Jenny's Blackie." Mandy said.

"Sorry," said James. "That lamb is amazing. He's fit as a fiddle, jumping all over the place. Mr. Spiller says he should have him set on in no time."

"So he's okay to go to the hospital tomorrow?" Mandy asked.

"No problem," said James.

Not for the lamb, Mandy thought. But getting in and out of the hospital unseen by the head nurse could be a big problem for them!

Twelve

Mary Anne's new nightgown was bright yellow with blue polka dots.

"Do you like it?" she said to Mandy and James.

"It'll break the cameras," James said.

Mary Anne's mouth turned down.

"James is only joking," Mandy said. "It's beautiful, Mary Anne."

"Well, it hurts my eyes just looking at it," James said.

"Shh," said Mandy. "We're depending on Mary Anne to let us in." She stood on tiptoe again to talk to the little girl through the open window of the children's ward.

"Remember, Mary Anne," she said. "As soon as the

coast is clear, come around and open the French windows, then we can bring Jenny's lamb in to see her."

Mary Anne nodded. "Jenny doesn't think you're telling the truth. Is he really in there?" she said, looking at the cat basket Mandy was carrying.

Mandy nodded. "You'll see him when we bring him in," she said.

"Okay," Mary Anne said in a whisper. She turned back into the room. "Somebody is coming," she said.

"You get back into bed," said Mandy. "We'll wait here." She indicated a bush out of sight of the ward windows.

"I feel like a criminal," James said.

Mandy sighed. "Never mind," she said. "All we have to do is slip in, show the lamb to Jenny, and slip out again. It won't take long."

"It sure won't," said James. "Not if the head nurse catches us. It'll be over in minutes — painfully."

"She won't catch us," said Mandy. "She and Grandma are getting interviewed now. It's just a matter of waiting until Nurse Williams is out of the way."

"*Psst!*" came a voice from the window.

Mandy and James looked up.

"Nurse Williams is in the storeroom," Mary Anne called softly.

"Okay then, open the windows," Mandy said.

Quickly she and James ran around to the French windows. There was the sound of a latch being lifted from inside and then Mary Anne was standing there.

"You're great, Mary Anne," Mandy said as she and James stepped into the ward.

Mandy turned to Jenny's bed. A tousled head turned toward her.

"Jenny," said Mandy. "Look who we've brought to see you." She opened the lid of the cat basket.

Jenny sat up, her eyes wide. "Blackie?" she said. "My very own Blackie?"

Mandy put the basket down on top of Jenny's bed.

"Let me see," said Mary Anne, wriggling in front of Mandy.

"Careful," said Mandy. "Don't frighten him."

"Oh, look," said Jenny, and she lifted the little woolly lamb out of the basket.

"Hi," said a voice from the other end of the room. "Don't forget me."

"I'll let Mary Anne bring him over to see you, Johnny," Jenny said.

Mandy opened her mouth to say no, but when she looked at Jenny's face she couldn't bear to. Instead of the white face and big, sad eyes, Jenny was the picture of happiness.

"Be quick," said Mandy. "We can't stay long."

Jenny handed the little lamb to Mary Anne and Mary Anne scurried across the ward with him.

"There," said Mary Anne, and she plonked the lamb down on Johnny's bed. Its black woolly legs splayed out on either side as the lamb tried to stand up.

"He's great," Johnny was saying when there was a sound in the corridor.

"Who's that?" asked Mandy.

Mary Anne rushed to the door.

"The head nurse!" she said. "And another lady and a man with a camera!"

"What?" said James. "Where are they going?"

Mary Anne darted back into the room. "I think they're coming here," she said.

Mandy dashed across the ward, grabbed the lamb, and thrust him into the cat basket. The footsteps were getting nearer. She looked across the ward. They would never get out without being seen. She backed toward the wall and found a door behind her.

"What's this?" she asked.

"I don't know," said Mary Anne.

Mandy pushed the door open. "Come on, James," she said. "Get back into bed, you two, and don't say a word!"

James got the door shut just in time.

They heard voices, and Nurse Williams said, "Look

who's here to see you, children. The head nurse. And this is Mr. Peters, who is going to take some pictures for television."

"Phew!" said James. "That was close!"

Mandy looked around. What they needed was a way out.

"What is this place?" James whispered.

Mandy looked at the machines. "It's the hospital laundry," she said. "Look, those are washing machines and dryers."

"They're a lot bigger than ours at home," said James.

"They would have to be," Mandy said. "And look at the big buckets of soap flakes."

"Like snow," James laughed.

Mandy frowned. There were windows in the room but they were high up, right next to the ceiling.

"It's okay," said James. "They won't come in here. Why on earth would they want to come into the laundry?"

At that, the door opened and the head nurse's voice said, "And this is the laundry!"

There was a scuffling sound inside the cat basket and the little black lamb leaped nimbly out.

"What on earth are you doing here, Mandy?" Grandma asked. Mandy whirled around to catch the lamb, missed, and gasped in horror as it skipped into one of the buckets of soap flakes.

Scrabbling for a foothold, the lamb kicked up clouds of soft white flakes that floated in the air before coming to rest all over the laundry room.

"A lamb?" asked Mr. Peters. "In the laundry?"

Then Blackie got a grip on the side of the bucket, and with a kick of his heels, he was free and scampering between the head nurse's feet and into the ward.

"Catch him!" said James.

"Is that an animal in my hospital?" cried the head nurse. "Another one?"

"Oh, Mandy," said Grandma.

In the background Jenny's voice could be heard calling to the lamb and Mary Anne was squealing with delight.

"Oh, Lord," said James. "We're really in for it now!"

Thirteen

The head nurse drew herself up and looked at Mandy and James.

"You can't be mad at them," said a small figure in a blue-and-yellow polka dot nightgown.

The head nurse looked down. "Mary Anne," she said. "Get back into bed at once."

"But they only did it to make Jenny better," said Mary Anne. "She wasn't getting better because she was worried about her little lamb. She's much better now. It isn't fair to blame Mandy and James. They rescued her and now they've made her better."

Mandy and James looked at her, aghast. They would never dare to speak to the head nurse like that.

Mr. Peters cut in before the head nurse could speak.

"What's this about a rescue?" he asked.

Mary Anne launched into her story. There was no stopping her once she got going. Not only that, but the story was growing as she told it. Mary Anne obviously had an amazing imagination.

"She's making half of it up," James said to Mandy. "Sounds good though, doesn't it?"

But Mandy was listening to Mary Anne and watching Mr. Peters. He had signaled to another man standing behind him, the man with the camera, and Mary Anne was being filmed while she spoke.

"This is a great story," Mr. Peters said.

At last Mary Anne ran out of steam and Mr. Peters looked beyond her at the ward.

"Hey, Phil," he said to the man with the camera, "get a shot of the little girl with the lamb, will you?"

Mandy looked. There was Jenny with Blackie in her arms. Only he wasn't totally black any longer. He was still covered in white soap flakes. Jenny was rubbing him down with a towel.

"Hey, this is a great idea," said Mr. Peters. "Just what we need — human interest. Pets in hospitals and all

that." He turned to the head nurse. "You know they're finding that sick people recover quicker if they have pets — especially children. You're really in the forefront of this, aren't you?"

For a long moment the head nurse didn't speak. She looked from Mandy and James standing among the soap flakes to Mary Anne clutching her doll to Johnny trying to sit up in bed to Jenny, her face wreathed in smiles, cuddling Blackie the lamb.

"Of course," she said to Mr. Peters. "Just because this is a small country hospital doesn't mean we aren't modern. And being so small," she added, "we can afford to be flexible. We can cater to the individual needs of all our patients."

Mandy felt her jaw drop.

"She's worse than Mary Anne!" James whispered in her ear.

Grandma was smiling broadly.

"And what's more," Grandma said, "we're going to adopt that little lamb for our campaign."

The head nurse turned to her and opened her mouth to speak. Then she closed it again.

"Terrific," said Mr. Peters. "Look." He took the head nurse aside. "I'm beginning to get a few ideas here. I mean, this stuff about animals helping people recover is pretty interesting. Say we combine your campaign with a story on how pets can aid recovery? I imagine we could get you pretty wide coverage." He scratched his chin. "Have you ever thought of having a pets' corner in the hospital?"

"Of course we have," said Grandma, winking at Mandy and James. "The head nurse and I were just talking about that, weren't we?"

The head nurse looked at Grandma, then she coughed. She looked across at Jenny, her head to one side. Mandy held her breath.

"You know," the head nurse said, "it's only when you see the difference this kind of thing can make to a child's recovery that you realize how important pets are to people." She turned to Mandy and James and smiled. "Some of us take longer to learn that than others," she said. "But it's a lesson not easily forgotten."

She turned back to the television crew. "Why don't you come to my office and we'll discuss your film? I think I can assure you that we are very seriously considering having a pets' corner at the hospital and I can think of two young people who would be ideal for running it." She turned back and looked at Mandy and James. "If they would take the job on," she said.

"Would we?" said Mandy.

"You bet!" said James.

*   *   *

"It's like a little coat," Jenny said.

Dr. Adam and Mandy looked at each other.

"That's just what it is," Dr. Adam said.

Mandy smiled at Jenny's description. No point in telling the little girl it was the skin of a dead lamb they were putting on Blackie. Instead she said, "It's called setting on. If we put this coat on Blackie, the ewe will think it's her own lamb and then she'll feed him."

"But I'll still be able to come up to the field to see him," Jenny said.

"Of course you will," said Mr. Spiller. "He's your lamb, isn't he?"

It was two weeks after the scene at the hospital and Jenny was her old self again. She had looked after Blackie carefully when she came home from the hospital but now it was time for the little lamb to be put with the others in the field — if they could find a substitute mother for him.

Jenny smiled happily as they watched the ewe nuzzle Blackie and sniff suspiciously. Mandy held her breath. If the ewe wasn't fooled by the smell of her own dead lamb's coat she would reject Blackie. The ewe sniffed again. Then she nudged Blackie toward her and the little lamb started to suckle.

Mandy breathed a sigh of relief.

"It worked!" said James.

"Like a dream," said Dr. Adam. "I think that's the last of your lambing problems, Jack."

Jack Spiller turned to him. "The end of my first lambing season. I couldn't have done it without your help," he said. "Not to mention these two and the people from Welford. They've been so good to us."

"Why wouldn't they be?" said Dr. Adam. "They're neighbors, aren't they?"

Jack Spiller smiled. "The best," he said. "I really feel as if I belong here now."

Dr. Adam laughed. "That's just as well," he said. "Because I was thinking of asking you to lend a hand at this year's Welford County Fair. And I thought you might enter Jess in the sheepdog trials."

"I'd be delighted," said Jack Spiller.

There was a shout from down the hill. Maggie Spiller was waving a newspaper and running up the hill toward them.

"What is it?" Jack Spiller said as she reached them.

"Look!" his wife said. "We're famous! At least Jenny's Blackie is."

Mandy and James craned to see what was on the front page of the paper.

The headline stood out:

LAMB SAVES HOSPITAL

"What?" asked Mandy.

Maggie Spiller laughed. "Yes," she said. "It's Blackie. The cottage hospital has had a reprieve. After that TV program went on, they had hundreds of letters and phone calls. Blackie's going to be the logo for a national campaign to save cottage hospitals."

"Hey," said James. "Your grandma will be happy."

Mrs. Spiller nodded. "It says here that Mrs. Dorothy Hope is going to be on the national committee."

"Good for Grandma," Mandy said. "Isn't that great, Dad?"

Dr. Adam ran a hand through his hair. "I just hope Grandpa can stand the pace," he said. Then he laughed. "Of course it's great. And I hope she saves lots more cottage hospitals."

"Oh, she will," said Mandy. "With a logo like that, how could she fail?"

She looked at the national campaign's logo. It showed a little black lamb clutched in the arms of a child. Then she looked at Jenny, who was absorbed in watching Blackie and his new mother.

The little girl looked up. "Blackie will always be my lamb, won't he?" she said.

Mandy knelt down beside her. "Of course he will, Jenny," she said. "Nobody loves him like you do."